"A courageous calling out, raising unc
about what mostly gets hushed up in our societies—the threat of abuse
and the act itself, the strangeness surrounding the ask for help, in short,
the emotional and often invisible labour of daily survival in a place
called 'home'. Perhaps most poignantly, whilst this carefully crafted
world complicates conversations around womanhood and privilege, it
isn't bereft of light and redemption."

—Saba Karim Khan, author of *Skyfall*

"The gently wrought story of a Pakistani family struggling through the
aftermath of an unimaginable tragedy. It addresses themes of loss, family,
womanhood and friendship with sensitivity, grace and an enduring love
for Pakistan."

—Cherie Jones, author of
How the One-Armed Sister Sweeps Her House

"The work of an innate storyteller, a riveting and moving tale, which
employs the perspective of several narrators, to advantage; it creates
with great sensitivity, the unexpected reverberations of sudden tragedy
on each individual. In the process it interweaves, past and present, the
memories of joy and suffering, friendships and exclusions. The novel
presents the complexities of trauma and mental aberrations with
particular skill, including the pressures of daily life, class and gender."

—Muneeza Shamsie, literary critic and author of
Hybrid Tapestries: The Development of Pakistani Literature in English

"Safinah Danish Elahi's energetic and graceful weaving together of
the lives, loves, joys and sorrows of the multiple characters this novel
embraces, is as playful at times, as it is moving. By the novel's conclusion,
I felt as if I had been on a deeply satisfying journey."

—Briar Grace Smith, script writer,
director, and member of the Academy of
Motion Picture Arts and Sciences (Oscars)

THE IDLE STANCE OF THE TIPPLER PIGEON

SAFINAH DANISH ELAHI

Neem Tree
Press

Published by Neem Tree Press Limited, 2023
Copyright © Safinah Danish Elahi, 2023

1 3 5 7 9 10 8 6 4 2

Neem Tree Press Limited
95A Ridgmount Gardens, London, WC1E 7AZ
United Kingdom
info@neemtreepress.com
www.neemtreepress.com

A catalogue record for this book is available from the British Library

ISBN 978-1-911107-70-5 Paperback
ISBN 978-1-911107-71-2 Ebook

Printed and bound in Great Britain

For Aleesha and Affaan

All children need love,
Even and especially,
The badly behaved ones.

PART 1

NADIA

Daylight dims outside my window, as I heave a sigh. I wrap up my work for the day. The electricity bills for this month are higher than they were last month. In fact, they are the highest in this quarter and I know Shadab *sahab* won't be pleased. I take one last look at the screen, hoping for the number to magically change so I won't have to face his piercing eyes again.

But I know I can only hope.

To say the persistence of his probing eyes makes me uncomfortable would be a gross understatement. I can feel his repulsive gaze on me every time I get up from my seat; I know he's watching me leave, X-raying my worn-out *shalwar kameez* from top to bottom. My mother once told me that I think of myself as some movie star: confident and perhaps deriving pleasure from the fact that people look at me wherever I go. But no, Amma, it's never that.

And this Shadab *sahab*? Well, I'm telling you, something about his gaze is just not right.

I quickly switch off the desktop, fix my headscarf, and put my mobile phone in my purse.

"Off already?" asks Faisal, smirking. He shifts from one foot to the other, scratching the salt and pepper stubble on his chin. "You girls really take the nine-to-five rule to heart, don't you? We fools have to stay back, and there is no talk of overtime. Ever."

Faisal began working at the office long before me, so, on account of his seniority, I don't usually respond as freely as I would like. He has a habit of commenting on everything that goes on: who comes, who goes. He may also be under the impression that I am his friend. Urgh. Not in this lifetime.

"I have to get home early. My husband isn't feeling well."

"Yes, husband, mother, child. Go on. Enjoy the weather while you're at it. This place needs some ventilation."

I scoff inwardly. Lahore, this time of the year, is hot and dry. The office is probably the cleanest and coldest place I spend time at, albeit with bad ventilation. Especially near the toilets.

When Faisal talks, it's like he's talking to himself. He doesn't even wait for the other person to reply. He has thin lips, almost like a hurried afterthought when he was being formed—though, it was the first thing I noticed about him. Someone at the office once said his fiancée left him for his best friend and he's never been the same since. Maybe she left because he's always been this irritating, I think now.

I walk past the receptionist, Uzma, slightly waving at her while heading towards the elevator. Her *dupatta* rests on her shoulder, her lips bright pink—the same hue she applies every day. Even though my office is located on the second floor, I'm careful to *never* take the stairs. No woman in her right mind wants to pass by that shady tuition centre, Indigo, and the strange guard who never misses an opportunity to scan women head to

4

toe with those penetrating eyes of his. He has a stare so sharp, my *kameez* feels shredded to nothing more than a spider's web by the time I've walked by. Some days, Mubashir picks me up from work—that is, if he is not sleeping. Most days, he passes out after finishing up one of his cheap bottles of local beer and wouldn't know if a dog shat on him. Talk about marrying low. Ah, well—I guess I had my reasons at the time. Ever since I was a child, I feared the police. I would have vivid nightmares about the *police waalas* coming to my house to arrest me.

Damp sheets, pattering fan, that terrible stench.

I would wake in the middle of the night shivering, not knowing where I was. It was all so frightening. When I met Mubashir, I found out that his dad was an influential *hawaldaar*. Funny how a few days can impact the decisions we make for the rest of our lives. I thought, What could be better than marrying a *police waala*'s son? As it turned out, I couldn't have been more wrong.

I reach the main gate and call Mubashir. If he answers, it means he is on his way to pick me up. If he doesn't, he is likely lying somewhere, dead to the world.

One ring…*Kisay da yaar na wichray*, sings the ringtone… two…three. Nope. Dead to the world it is.

I start to walk towards the Main Boulevard, hoping to catch a rickshaw—a rare sight in Gulberg. I think of getting an Uber, but spending so much on a ride is something that never made sense to me.

Tucking my purse under my arm, I wave my free hand at a rickshaw coming towards me. "*Bhai, bhai*, stop."

The rickshaw comes to an abrupt halt near me. The driver flashes a paan-laden toothy smile, not taking his eyes off me for a single second.

"Where to, *baji*?"

"Naulakha Bazar."

"That'll be 250 rupees."

"*Chal!* I won't give a rupee over 100."

"*Acha*, 150. Come, sit."

The truth is, most rickshaw drivers don't really know about the small locality I live in, so I just get dropped off around the nearby Shaheed Ganj Mosque. It is only a ten-minute walk home from there, and, if it's evening time, the streets are emptier, cleared of the chance of being harassed. The rickshaw engine sputters, bringing it to life. Faraway, a siren wails.

I remember my life in sounds. The sound of my mother's ladle clinking against the saucepan. The chirping of mynahs in the fields just as the early morning breeze would begin to blow. The sound of Mrs. Farid's metal ruler on my palm. The way Misha's bracelets clanked against each other, Misha's laughter, Misha's…

Okay, let's not go there.

Truthfully, I can't really complain about my life. No one in my family thought I would become this *memsahab*, working in a fancy office. Especially after enduring what the Hashims put me through. They may have propelled me onto an upward path of some social mobility by enabling me to acquire an education, but I don't think much of myself. I was plucked from homes too abruptly—both mine and the Hashims'—leaving me disorientated and detached from both ways of life. Everyone now, however, sees this job and, well, let's just say no one in my family has had an office job before—if you don't count cousin Iftikhar, who worked as a peon.

When life is giving you lemons, all you need is to squeeze them really hard to make the best lemonade possible. If you can afford a fridge, *jee*, then refrigerate it for a little while. There is nothing better than chilled lemonade, especially in the scorching heat of Lahore.

That is what I did with all the lemons life gave me, no matter how many. I worked hard, kept my head high, and marched on, regardless of what life threw at me. And look where I am now. I could have been sweeping floors, cleaning someone's dirty toilets, but instead, I have my own computer to work on, a decent job, and a roof over my head that I pay for with my own money.

I just wish Mubashir also brought something to the table, so we could live in a proper apartment, and not this shabby quarter that we must make do with right now. But, I remind myself, let's take life as it comes, one lemon at a time, shall we?

ZOHAIB

London, United Kingdom

Dr. Whitaker slides his wire-rimmed glasses to the bridge of his nose and peers at me.

"So, how are we doing this Friday? Big plans for the weekend…?"

"No, doctor; you know I don't go out that mmmuch—it's too cold."

"Then wear your coat and go. You know staying home at the weekend is not a good idea. Plus, didn't you tell me your parents were planning to visit?"

"Baba was going to…I think I forgot to tell you. Baba's visa expired. And now he needs to get it renewed and I can't meet them till he does."

"What about your mum?"

"She…well…"

"Hmm, it's all right. Soon, then." Dr. Whitaker furrows his brows.

"Yeah," I say curtly. "Mama has been saying she'll come, but she keeps delaying it. Though, I do feel it would do my sister good—she really could use the company. You know, Misha really misses them."

I look around the spacious room, sunlight seeping through the tall windows and white blinds. It reminds me of the patio at 55 Alhamra, although the view outside is starkly different from the view there. 55 Alhamra was my sanctuary. My safe place. The pink plumeria flowers that one could always see, fallen to the ground as if someone had carefully placed them there to be photographed. Instead, the clinic sits atop a four-storey building, tucked away from the hubbub of Harley Street where the city's hustle and bustle can be heard more audibly. Dr. Whitaker's clinic has become my second home.

I have been seeing him since I moved here. He's like my father, only older, and whiter.

"Anyway, did I tell you the heating in my apartment hasn't been working for a week?"

"Have you called the landlord? Perhaps you could inform someone…What was his name? Mike?"

"I-I-I…"

"It's just a suggestion, but, in this weather, don't you think it would be wise to get it fixed? I'm sure the building's supervisor will take in your complaint and get it fixed in no time."

I don't like the supervisor, Mike. He asks me too many questions.

"I have to go," I respond.

Dr. Whitaker shifts in his seat.

I make no attempt to actually leave.

"Okay, how about you tell me about that girl you liked at work? What was her name? Cecilia? Cici, you were calling her."

"Yes, but Misha didn't like her because she swore in front of her. I didn't like that either, so I just told her to get out of my life."

"That seems a little drastic, to push her out of your life for swearing. Could you not have expressed to her how you felt about her language? Do you think you were falling into the old habit we talked about last time? You know, when you said that you find excuses to push people out of your life—do you think you may be doing that here?"

"But I just told you…"

Behind him, his degrees shine like frost in the moonlight. *Post Graduate Lecturer. Consultant Psychiatrist, London Psychology Centre.* Some awards I can't quite read clearly. I draw my attention back to Dr. Whitaker's face. Deep worry lines are sketched on his forehead. His expression is gentle.

I look around to search for the time. I stopped wearing a watch a few years ago, when I was mugged coming out of Tottenham Court Road station. The doctor had a huge clock removed from the wall because the ticking made me anxious. But I keep looking at the spot where the clock used to be, during our earliest sessions. Not seeing it on the wall also makes me anxious. As do 1,029,735 other things.

"She seemed like a nice girl. Why don't you tell me what really bothered you about her?"

"I told you, doc. She wasn't a 'nice girl'. Oh, you know my mum sent me pictures of some girls. It was hilarious. Misha and I laughed until our bellies ached. Mum actually told me to choose one to marry!"

"Well, I understand it is a perfectly acceptable way of looking for a partner, in some South Asian cultures. Perhaps you could give it a try, too?"

I can't believe my doc wants me to consider an arranged marriage. My parents spend £130 a session to have this buffoon convince me I should marry someone I've never met. Bravo.

I didn't mean to call him a buffoon. He's like my dad. But, come on.

"Doc, seriously? How can you tell me to even consider it? They're just trying to make me come back to Pakistan, now. What's the point of mmmarriage, if one day it's all going to fall apart, anyway?"

"You know very well that all marriages don't end up like that."

"Mama and Baba's did," I say quietly.

I look down at my shoes. I tap my right foot ferociously. I don't want to talk anymore; my head suddenly feels heavy, like it has been filled with grey clouds, dark and angry. I feel grief in my toes, my knees. I can feel it winding up my body. I stand up abruptly.

"Let's take it from here, next week," Dr. Whitaker says, looking up from his notes. "I want you to maybe think back to a time when your parents were there for you. Together."

I close my eyes for a moment. Baba holding his hand in mine. The early morning Karachi breeze, humid and salty, waves crooning a deep rumble as we walk along the shore. Mama, cocooned in her emerald-green shawl—her eyes downward, she smiles her beautiful radiant smile. I miss that smile.

I jerk my eyes open. Right. Whitaker's clinic.

"O-okay, doc. See you next week."

I grab my satchel, and off I go through the door. I don't have to pay for my sessions because Baba transfers money directly into the doc's account. Plus, I'd never be able to afford him on top of the yoga and meditation classes Talha makes me sign up for. I step into the small reception where Dr. Whitaker's PA sits. Technically, he isn't a shrink, but I just like saying that. As I amble down the stairs, I take my thoughts with me. I don't take the elevator. It's too small and dark, and I don't like being restricted in compact, enclosed spaces.

Talha is to me what London has been for many: a haven for the homeless. I found him the year I moved here. Although originally from Pakistan, he hardly has any memories of the place. He told me once his parents are from Sialkot, the city of football factories. Talha was quite the shock to my family's sensibilities. Not that there has been much interaction between him and my parents, to be honest. It was just a few times he was around on the odd occasions they've visited over the years. In our teens, his bleached-blond hair and nose ring were too much of a shock for Baba and his traditional ways. It angered me then, but amuses me now. Talha hasn't changed, forever comfortable in who he is.

We did our GCSEs together. Despite being the only other brown boy in our class, I wasn't immediately drawn towards him. He was artistic and chatty, while I was sullen and withdrawn. But, when I noticed him getting picked on by some of the other boys one day after school, something visceral inside me stirred and I found myself rallying to his side. From that day on, we were inseparable. I would go around to his house when I missed Mama. Farzana Aunty, a petite woman with a round face, would quickly make a fresh round *roti* and fetch my favourite kebabs, which she'd save for me. Some days, when we had the afternoon to ourselves, Talha and I would go around on our bikes and grab all-you-can-eat pizza—he liked the greasy pizza joint. But it's not all me rescuing him; he's rescued me, too. He has this way of calming me down whenever I have a dark episode. He's a good guy, Talha.

I get myself out onto the street, and, for a second, I forget where I am. Right, the doc's clinic. I need to get home. For that, I need to take the Tube. The sky is a clear blue, but, in the distance, I can see the sun ready to make its exit. Go, dude—you leave, too. I pick up my pace as I head towards Regent's Park station. I need to be home for Misha.

MISHA

Karachi, Pakistan

Nono and I have been best friends since I was, like, two years old. That's, like, so many years ago. I was a baby when she came to our house. The best part is that she lives in my house. Whattt? Yes! How cool is it to have your best friend live with you? She came so long ago that I can't imagine my life without her. She can be just as naughty as me sometimes, and, other times, a saint, an angel.

Anyway, today I've told her we're going to go check out the *maulvi sahab*'s quarters. It's a bit scary there, but it will be so fun. She says she needs to ask her mum before going, but I know how to convince Masi because she never says no to me. I have a ton of homework to do because I didn't do it before—after lunch, I mean. Nono has done hers, which is unfair because her school gives almost no homework, but I reckon mine is going to take only fifteen minutes or so. I only have to write ten sentences. And there's some maths work. Anyway, I'm about to go check on Nono when Mama calls me and asks me if I've done my homework. Oomph. I run from there so I can drown her voice out. Nono

13

usually hangs around the veranda after Masi is done with her work, so that's where I'm headed.

"Nono!" I whisper.

"Yes, what?" she smirks.

She finds it funny that I call her Nono instead of Nadia. She got this nickname because, when she first came to our house, she only knew how to say "no" in English, so, whatever we would ask her, she would just reply with, "No, no." Mama found this very funny. So, all of us started calling her Nono.

"*Chalo!* Remember our plan?"

"Yes, but I don't want to go. You get me into trouble." She makes a face at me.

"Come on. You promised. Okay, you didn't promise, but can you please for once stop being a scaredy-cat?" I say, not taking no for an answer.

"Okay, but we need to be back before dark. You know, *na*, the *maulvi sahab*'s quarters are haunted."

"Why else do you think we're going?" I say with a wry smile.

I take her hand and we skip down the stairs. The staircase has a banister which we usually slide down, but you have to be a little careful with the slide and right now I am in a hurry. The *maulvi sahab* is out teaching, so we must take this chance to get into his empty quarters. I'm not sure what my plan is, but ideas usually just come to me, like, in the middle of my plans, and they're pretty good and fun, even if I say so myself.

"Slow down! I'll fall!" Nono shrieks.

"You won't!" I scream back, my hair flying.

We reach the bottom step and I pull her hand towards the main door. As we walk out, we hear the *azan*. I don't know which prayer time it's calling for, because I only know the *Zuhr* prayer. I prayed it last month with my half-*roza*. We run towards the quarters at the back of our house, where the hens are usually kept. It smells of poop and stale food, and I wonder what the chickens eat. Akbar *chacha* looks after them and gives us their eggs, which look a little bit different from the ones we buy at the store. I don't know exactly how different they are in taste, because I've only ever eaten cooked ones.

We run and run—on the concrete, through the garden, the damp grass grazing our bare feet, the light fading into darkness. It must be the *azan* that turns the day into night, but I have more important things to think about right now. That is, to figure out if the *maulvi sahab* is human or one of those ghost things—*djinns*, they're called. Once, Masi told me a story about *djinns* in her village, and since then I have made it my mission to find out more about them. She told me about one woman whose feet were backwards, a sure sign that she was actually a *djinn*, and she could still walk perfectly with her back-to-front feet. I've checked on people's feet ever since. And there was a man in her village who would come and go without making the slightest sound. Like a ghost! Except he was a *djinn*, too. The *maulvi sahab*, with his small size and big beard, is someone who could be connected to the *djinn*, I reckon.

"Nono! Here, quick—hide here," I say, ducking behind a wall. Even though I am kind of still visible, it is better than being caught by the *maulvi sahab*'s partner *djinns*.

"I don't want to go. I want to go back. *Chalo, na*, it's getting dark," she says timidly.

I ignore her and walk towards the quarters of the *maulvi sahab*'s house. Mosquitoes buzz in my ear and I make a half-hearted attempt to swat at them. I am so close; I cannot turn back now. Nono is such a scaredy-cat. No fun. I suck in my breath to stop smelling the yucky poop air. I step over some trash—

discarded milk cartons; the *maulvi sahab* doesn't seem to have kept the alley very clean outside his room; I wonder if he ever gets the time to. I just need to peek into the quarters and see. Once I see the place from the inside, I'm pretty sure I'll just *know*.

Nono catches up with me and we hold hands, fingers entangled, walking slowly towards the house. The *azan* was a while ago, so it's quite dark now. He will be back soon, and, if he catches us, he will definitely tell Baba.

Just then, I hear a *very* loud scream! Am I screaming? No, I'm pretty sure my mouth is closed. I see a shadow of the *djinn* moving quickly towards us. And I hear another loud scream! This time, I'm pretty sure it's mine.

NADIA

Mubashir is passed out on the *charpoy*, his one arm dangling off the metal rod where the strings have ripped and formed a hole. His hair is dirty, and saliva is dribbling from his mouth. I sigh and put my worn-out faux-leather purse on the kitchen counter. Since the quarter we live in is so small, I can enter and reach the kitchen counter in about six steps. The kitchen, living area and washing area are all within the same space, occupying different corners, off which is the one bathroom we have. I feel like, no matter how much I clean up, it still faintly smells of urine in here. It's a pretty small colony we live in. Of course, once Mubashir finds work, we will upgrade our living conditions. People in my office would never believe I live in this filth, but what can I do? Mubashir squanders away all my money on his *nasha*.

"Tsk, tsk." I click my tongue just looking at Mubashir and pull up my *shalwar* a little, so my clothes don't get *napaak* from the water—or possibly piss—outside the toilet. I need a quick bath before I deal with Mr. Dead-to-the-World. I take off my clothes and carefully hang them on the doorknob, so I can put them back on after my bath. I fill the orange plastic bucket with cold water and scramble around for a cup to pour water over my body. When I realize it's not there, I pick up the bucket, now heavy with the weight of water, and dump it on my head.

He really didn't have to be like this.

He wasn't, when I married him.

It seems like another lifetime, but it was only four years ago that I met him. He was clean and charming, with kohl in his eyes and that lopsided grin that used to be endearing. He would follow me from outside my college and we would meet for a mango drink in the scorching heat of the Lahori summer. I had recently moved to Lahore, escaping the bleakness of my previous life. We got married right after I finished my BA. I wanted to rent an apartment, but Mubashir said he wanted to work some more before we chose a place. "We should save up," he had said, "get a bigger place for our kids." That's when it really hit me what marriage was going to be like. I'm not particularly fond of children. It's not that I don't like them; it's just that I remember all too well my own childhood, when all of *that* happened. I had told myself I'd never burden myself with the responsibility of a child in a world that allows such awful things to happen to them. A world where adults become just as vulnerable, or callously look away. I did what I thought would save me the argument: I told him I was incapable of having children. I blamed it on some childhood sickness and—as is typical of most men—he wanted to be spared any details that might involve the female anatomy, so I got away with saying very little. It was almost funny, really.

But Mubashir had always wanted to have children. At the time, I thought I was saving myself from disaster, but now I sometimes wonder if my decision not to have them was what pushed him into becoming this useless junkie. Whatever the reasoning, it seems disaster was my destiny, whichever path I decided to take.

He grunts in his sleep. What demons have him in their grip as he dreams? His foot is bruised from last week when he claimed to have gone in search of a job with the local street cobbler. Apparently, he hurt his foot trying to hammer a nail in a shoe. To be honest, it sounds like a load of *chuna*, and he thinks I'm dumb enough to believe that story. I just want to shake him sometimes, remind him what life could have been for us. Before he became this—this useless addict. Maybe I could share an apartment with Uzma from reception. She's single, I think. Men in our office ogle her just like they ogle me, but I think I'm a bit prettier because my skin is fairer. All that Olivia cream I have been spending money on over the years. Olivia, really *shukriya*. Not that it has made a difference in my life. I don't even appreciate anyone looking at my skin. I would even don the niqab, but I'd probably get pimples on my face and who wants that?

No, if Mubashir would just release himself from his vices, we could rent a portion, in a ten-*marla* house in Johar Town. And the view, *aray*, the view would be fantastic, not like this garbage that we live in. And it would be mosquito-free. Already the mosquitoes are so terrible, and, lately, the dengue epidemic has scared me even more. I can't afford the weeks of hospital bills you need to pay to get your platelets up. Maybe I could just leave him. He wouldn't even notice, if it weren't for all the money I have been investing in this so-called marriage. That's the thing: I can't. I just can't. Not after all the people I ever cared about left me. Still, thoughts of leaving him arise more frequently, these days, and the struggle to block them becomes harder each time. But I do block them away, for one more day.

MISHA

Karachi, Pakistan

Bhai is back from attending Friday prayers with Baba and should be ready to set up shop. Back from the mosque means he will put up his mini bazaar for all of us. Baba told me all our cousins come over to our house for Friday lunch because he's the eldest brother and we have the biggest dining table. I don't think the dining-table part is true, because my cousin Anaya definitely has a bigger house, so they must have a bigger dining table too, but I don't say anything to Baba. It doesn't really matter if it's true or not because I like it when my cousins come over. The only thing I don't like is that Mama doesn't let Nono sit with us, and that's not fun at all because she has to eat with Masi in the kitchen and I can't discuss my plan of how I will convince Bhai to give me a discount on the *chorun* he gets from Ameer *bhai*'s shop near the mosque. I will bargain with him and offer to let him use my stationery set for a week—the one Amal gave me as a present last year on my birthday—because it's not even girly and Bhai can use the sticky notes for all his fat textbooks from school. But Nono usually tells me how to deal with Bhai—she has a way of

20

making him listen to her. Like the time she had Bhai take us to the *makai wala o*n the street corner. Mama never lets us step outside, but Bhai is allowed to go. And, just last week, Nono had somehow convinced Bhai to take us with him. I don't really know what she says to him because Bhai usually does not like it when I ask to tag along.

I quickly brush my hair and fix my frock—it's frilly at the bottom, with butterflies all over it, pink and purple, two of my most favourite colours. I can hear Baba discussing something important with Anaya's dad. I want to check how big Bhai's bag is, to see how much I can get with the thirty rupees I have been saving all week. Mama gives me five or ten rupees change whenever she gets her groceries from the market, and I try to collect coins and ten-rupee notes if they are left on the counter or her dressing table. And then I save and save in my piggy bank, and on Friday I buy however many things I can from Bhai, hoping to persuade him to give me good deals.

If Nono gets a chance, she definitely gets a good deal from Bhai. Later, we sit on the veranda and eat our *chorun* and candies.

The bag is not that big today. Don't know what is up with that, but I feel the coins and notes in my hand and hop towards Bhai before Ali and Anaya start throwing their pocket money at him. I really don't understand why I don't get regular pocket money and they do. I mean, Ali is even shorter than me. Yeah, I know he's eight and I'm seven, but I'm a little taller than him, so, really, I deserve pocket money, too.

Nono stumbles in, carrying a jug of water too big for her, and gives Bhai a shy smile. Hello, I'm also here. I fake a cough. She looks at me and grins widely.

"Put it here, this side," Mama says to her, pointing towards one side of the dining table. Mama doesn't look at Nono, but

Nono knows she is being spoken to. She does what is asked of her, ducks her head, and quickly leaves the room.

"Bhai, Bhai, did you get *chorun*?" I whisper to Bhai, who is wearing a crisp white *shalwar kameez*. He's always trying to look taller when he's around adults, widening his shoulders, raising his eyebrows like Baba when he's in a serious conversation.

"Shh—not now," he says, following something Baba is talking about. Tomato prices going up or something. So boring.

I try again after a few minutes.

"Bhai, I want *chorun*; I can buy all of it, so you don't have to deal with so much maths. I'll give you twenty rupees for a pack of twelve. What do you say? *Haan*?"

Bhai looks over at me dismissively, shaking his foot under the table.

"You can also use my stationery," I say, using my secret weapon.

"What? No, I didn't bring any *chorun* today," he says, looking over at me for a second.

Oh, noooo—this is so disappointing! I've been waiting all week. I want to wail, but I push a little more.

"Okay, thirty rupees for the pack of twelve," I say desperately, hoping it was just a price issue.

"I don't have it, dumbo," he scoffs.

Aaaaargh! Bhai can be such a meanie pants.

I flick my finger on his thigh and run away from the table. So unfair. He doesn't even tell us where this Ameer *bhai*'s shop is. Once, I drove around with Rasheed *chacha* trying to find this mystery shop, and I just couldn't find it. Maybe Bhai lied to us that it's near the mosque. I really don't want to wait another week! Maybe if I offer him a head massage with the stationery…

I know Mama is going to be calling out my name soon because I haven't finished my *daal chawal*, but I just want to plan something with Nono and figure out how we can find Ameer *bhai*'s shop.

The veranda is small but open-air—Masi does the washing there as well. It's my favourite place because it's usually where Nono and I hang out. Nono sometimes helps Masi sort out the clothes, but right now she is sitting cross-legged, bent over, looking at something. I'm so sad, but don't want to miss out on creeping up on her. She always gets scared and it makes me laugh so much!

I come up behind her slowly, imagining I'm a lion on the prowl, and then I jump, shouting, *"Boo!"*

She screams and spills something on the floor.

When I look down, I see lots and lots of coloured crystals of my all-time favourite *chorun*.

23

ZOHAIB

London, UK

I usually only stutter when I'm nervous. Not that Whitaker makes me nervous. It's more the knowledge that the conversation is really him trying to make sense of me—unpuzzle my mind, my life—which unnerves me. It becomes more than my body or senses can bear and my stutter emerges.

I only have a part-time job because Whitaker suggested I get one to get out of the house and occupy my mind. Not that I need the money. Not that the money is great. But it works because I can be home with Misha most of the time still. Whitaker also suggested it would be healthy to have the time away from Misha. I think my sister would pop by school too, if she could, but that's not possible, so she waits for me to get home and eagerly listens to how my day was.

Misha moved in with me when I finished business school at the University of West London. It was a gruelling three years. I couldn't have got through it without Talha next to me. I also know that Talha would never have chosen UWL, because his interests were in sports science, but he claimed he wanted to stay in London to save on accommodation costs and that he needed a more "practical degree", according to his parents, so he chose to do the same course as me. I was never sure about this claim, especially given how supportive Aunty and Uncle have been of some of Talha's most unorthodox choices, but I wasn't complaining. I graduated, just about, and even managed to get a job at the uni's orientation department. Somehow, that didn't work out for too long. I felt more and more concerned for Misha.

This is my first job since leaving the orientation department, and this time it's at a primary school. I don't interact much with the children—I just do some admin work, basic filing, form filling, issuance of IDs, that kind of stuff. It's not a bad place to work, but the parents really do live up to the stereotype of pompous private-school parents. But that's hardly surprising. I guess I just see it with more clarity now that I'm on the admin side of the school, rather than at a pupil's desk. Cecilia is one of the teachers here.

Her friends call her Cici. I think she's beautiful. She has the most gorgeous blond hair I've ever come across—not the dirty yellow kind, but a shade that reminds you of fresh honey; it almost invites you to feel it, to taste it even. Her hair complements her warm hazel eyes that seem to be carrying the world in them.

She is not a foul-mouthed woman. She hasn't even met Misha, because she's never been to my apartment. And to be honest, I have only spoken to her once in the staffroom, when I asked her to pass me a coaster for my coffee mug. She smiled this perfect smile and said the three most beautiful words I have ever heard in my life: "Sure, I can."

Cici has a little sister who is a pupil at the school. There's something in her precocious manner that reminds me of Misha. Every so often, I imagine all of us hanging out together—a dream

I wish would come true. Every time I look at them together, something tugs at my heart.

The truth is, I haven't had the courage to talk to too many girls here. They're very nice and want to be friends with me—maybe even more—but it's a bit complicated. I have never really fallen in love, or so I tell myself on the days I am convinced that childhood love doesn't count. But a childhood love, it's pure, that feeling—unadulterated, when there is only one person who inhabits your thoughts. It's the best kind of friendship: an understanding so deep it doesn't even require conversing. I shake my head, clearing it of these frivolous thoughts.

I push aside a huge file of student folders and check the time on my phone. I have three more hours of work left and then I can head back to the flat. Even though I need to get the heating fixed, the flat is the only place I feel completely safe. The streets sometimes confuse me, as though they conspire and move around behind my back each time I turn away. Even the weather feels harsh, as if it's punishing me too. Sometimes, I'm not able to communicate how I'm feeling: if I feel angry or upset, I find myself trapped inside this unfettered rage. There are times it leaves me trembling on the floor, crying. Yes, I'm a mess, but who isn't? Talha tells me to own myself, to engage my inner strength, to break free from the shackles of self-doubt and embrace my truth. As inspiring as Talha is, his new-age spirituality is not for me. Plus, he is easy-going, sociable and likeable. He doesn't need to make an effort to fit in; he doesn't need to control his anxiety in public; he doesn't have these *feelings* to deal with. Even when he was going through a tough time in his teens, his parents supported him, understood his predicament. Aunty and Uncle embrace Talha as his whole self. He has never needed to consider which part of him could be the cause of their abandonment, rejection or shame. There are no awkward silences, no pauses in their conversations. They can even go days without checking in on Talha, but it creates no distance in their relationship.

Meanwhile, both Mama and Baba call me regularly to "check up" on me, though we never get beyond the superficial enquiries: How am I doing? What have I eaten? How is work going? Have I made any friends? Even trying to probe for a possible girlfriend. They literally never ask about Misha, when I think she is the one they should be concerned about. They're old now, so I don't blame them that much, and they don't live together anymore, so it's almost like I'm answering the same question twice a day, just to different people. They always insist my move to London was to "shelter me," so I could "find myself," but, to be honest, I don't think I've ever felt more lost.

The yoga doesn't help either, and yet Talha wants to take me to a yoga retreat in Bali, where apparently you "self-evolve" and do intuitive therapy and reiki, or some shit. But I haven't committed to him or anything. If I mention it to Baba, he will go right ahead and book it for me, but I'm just not sure yet. Besides, what will I do about Misha? I can't leave her. I can't fail her, not again. Not ever again.

NADIA

Lahore, Pakistan

"I checked the bills at least twice. Maybe there is some mistake from Lesco's side? We had two different meters for the two floors, and it doesn't seem like we used any additional electronics."

I try to keep my eyes levelled on Shadab *sahab*'s desk while I brief him about the electricity bills. I never want to look at his face. I am repulsed by that sleazy, unnecessary grin and those prying eyes, raking every inch of my body with their laser-sharp intensity.

"Show these to me," he says, gesturing at the papers in my hand.

He brushes his hand against mine, lets it linger for a second too long, and I know this is not a mistake or a coincidence because it happens *every time* I'm in his office. I remember telling Uzma about it. She had dismissed it with a speedy, "He does this to everyone."

"How can you say that?" I asked her incredulously.

"It's harmless," she said to me curtly. She had looked around uneasily, her gaze resting on her lap, her back straight. I knew that was the end of the conversation.

Harmless? What nonsense! It harms *me*. I don't like how it makes me *feel*. But I know I can't quit, because it's a decent enough job. It pays well; it helps me keep a roof over my head. And, with how things are going with Mubashir, I can't risk being unemployed. What is it they always say? Better the devil you know.

"Yes, looks like it's a problem from their end," he says, looking at his watch. "Why don't you call them and come to my house later, tell me what they say? I'm heading to a meeting with Director *sahab* right now."

"Sir, I can call you and tell you what they say," I suggest, obviously trying to avoid the situation.

"No, you must explain to me in person. I need a paper trail, so bring me all the bills from last year as well. We can't let them do this to us."

"Sir, my husband is not feeling well." I know, hardly imaginative. I use this excuse all the time, but I feel cornered and need a way out of going to Shadab *sahab*'s house.

"Nadia, can you stop being *kaamchor*. It will only take half an hour. I need all details by six p.m. I'll be home around that time."

My head hums with possible excuses. He asked me once before to come to his house. Thankfully, Khursheed *sahab* had offered to take the papers on my behalf that time. A kind man, he had intervened with the skill of a seasoned diplomat, saving me from the discomfort of what might happen and saving Shadab *sahab* any embarrassment. But, this time, I don't seem to have any escape. Maybe Shadab *sahab* shouldn't be spared the embarrassment. I must avoid this. Maybe I will ask Mubashir to wait outside on his bike. At least I will have the possibility of rescue. Rescue? What am I thinking? Sure, he has a wandering eye, but Shadab *sahab* is married and has children, I believe. He

29

can't be planning anything inappropriate. I quietly nod my head and agree to his demand.

Stop being kaamchor—I hate that phrase, and for some reason it seems to follow me. The cook, Shah Zaman, used to say it to me all the time. When Amma wasn't around, he would ask me to clean the black granite counters, then nonchalantly make me work next to him. Some days, he would hold my arm and show me how the counters were to be cleaned. Other days—well, other days are a bit foggy, but I do remember him telling me he gets so tired and needs a massage.

I can feel the hair on my arms rise in protest. Sweat gathers on my upper lip as my mind takes me back to his moist palms against my bony elbow. The slow, intentional guide to sweeping, and my body going stiff against his deliberate instructions. "This way," he would say, pressing his body forcefully on my malleable torso. His hands grazing my shoulder, travelling down, gripping me, grabbing me. I blink my eyes rapidly to halt any tears.

A sharp pain rises in my gut; I clutch my stomach and press it, hoping that will make the pain go away. I can almost taste it, this horrific throb. I visited a doctor a few years ago and he suggested I get some tests done, but they were ridiculously expensive. I couldn't justify the cost; it's not like my stomach is hurting all the time. Right now, though, my main concern is collecting these bills for Shadab *sahab*. I won't be getting a saviour in a cape to avenge any of my difficulties. My job I'd like to keep, thank you.

MISHA

I'm tired and my feet are aching. Mama suggests I ask Nono to give me a massage, but I can't ask my best friend for a massage. That would be weird. I know I can't really say that to Mama, or she'd begin with her never-ending lecture on how Nono is not my best friend and how I should look for friends in school who are my age—someone like Myra or Ariana, not "some maid's daughter." But I don't understand Mama's behaviour with Nono. Although she pays for Nono's school and buys her school uniform for her, she never lets her sit with me or Bhai on the sofa, or even have Rasheed *chacha* drive her to school. She has a school van that comes to pick her up and drop her off. Once, I asked Mama if we could pick Nono up from school, but she refused and even seemed a little angry that I'd asked. I don't know what the problem is. I want Mama to start seeing Nono the way I see her: as one of us.

I want Nono to sleep in my room tonight. When I ask Mama, she says there is no extra bed, so she will have to sleep on the floor. In her own quarters, Nono has a *charpoy*, but she shares it with

31

Masi, and obviously I can't have them both sleep next to me in the space beside my bed. I ask Nono if she's okay with sleeping on the floor.

"On one condition." She smiles at me.

"Okay, what?" I ask, wary.

"I want that unicorn bracelet your Baba got you from America."

"Hey, it's new! And I love it…" My voice trails off.

"Okay, then—no, I don't want to sleep on the floor." She purses her lips. I know there is no way out of this.

"Fine, you can have it. But…well…" I sigh, resigned. "Nothing." I hand the bracelet over to her.

Her eyes instantly light up and she quickly puts it on her left wrist. It sparkles when she twists her arm this way and that. I am almost regretting giving her my bracelet, but I tell myself that I'll just ask Baba to get me another one. I will have to wait a few months, but, this time, I'll ask him to get me two: one unicorn and one rainbow.

She sets up her blanket on the floor and places a dirty pillow on it. She is taller than me; her feet stick out, showing her cracked heels. Ew, I should tell her to wash more.

"Hey, you'll be cold. The AC will be on," I tell her instead. I don't want to hurt her feelings and make her sad enough to not agree to this.

"I don't have two blankets." She makes a face.

This seems to be more complicated than I had first thought.

"She can have mine," bellows Bhai from his bed.

"Bhai, are you sure Mama will be okay with it?" I peer over to his side of the room.

Bhai shrugs. Maybe all twelve-year-old boys have this annoying habit of shrugging all the time.

I shrug back.

Suddenly, I don't feel so well. Maybe the pasta was too heavy? I knew there was something off about the sauce. Shah Zaman *chacha* usually adds a squirt of ketchup to make the sauce a bit orange, but today he tried another recipe. The sauce was white, and it just didn't feel right in my tummy.

I lie on my back. Nono is lying next to me on the floor, her blanket under her and Bhai's blanket over her. Her head rests on the dirty pillow.

I turn to Bhai's side. He is reading a book.

My stomach grumbles like a volcano erupting. I turn over to Nono's side now.

"Aah," I say. And, the next thing I know, I am retching. The vomit keeps flowing out of my mouth, flowing everywhere, finding its way towards Nono's makeshift bed. She's now covered in puke: her hair, arms, even Bhai's blanket.

"Sorry! *Bleughh*...Sorry, Nono..." I say, in between bouts of vomiting.

"You twit!" Bhai jumps up. He tries to pull away his blanket. He looks like he might throw up, too.

I know he's going to be super mad. I've thrown up over his blanket. He's never going to sell *chorun* to me again. He will tell Mama and Baba I had two chocolates from the fridge and never finished dinner on Tuesday. Oh, oh, oh!

It feels like the room is spinning. I think I'm falling down a deep, dark, spiralling hole. It twists and turns; it almost never ends.

When I open my eyes again, I see Nono being led to the washroom by Bhai. She turns around, with vomit in her hair and that cold look in her eyes. She lets Bhai take her hand.

That's the last thing I remember.

33

I wake up in Mama's room the next morning. I know because her paisley curtains are the first thing I catch a glimpse of when I open my eyes. My throat feels dry, and I try to reach for a glass on the side table. My hand touches something by the glass. My sight is still hazy, so I bring it closer to my face: Nono has returned my unicorn bracelet. Any other day, I would've felt happy about the turn of events. But, right now, I just feel so sad.

MISHA

Karachi, Pakistan

"Do you see that bird, Misha?" Baba asks, pointing to a string of pigeons lined up on the thick electric wires connected to the poles.

"Baba, those are pigeons! Not birds," I say, coyly, as if I know so much more than him.

"Well, yes, a pigeon is a kind of bird. And do you know what kind of pigeons those are?"

"I don't know—grey pigeons?"

"Haha! Yes, Misha—grey pigeons, that's the perfect type! Such a dodo you are," Bhai says, jeering.

"So? Grey pigeon can be a type of pigeon…What are you, a bird scientist?" I retort.

"Bird scientist? You mean *ornithologist*!" Bhai keels over, laughing.

"Hey, hey, *bachey*—don't make me regret bringing you guys here," Baba says sternly, his thick eyebrows raised in mock anger.

"They're sort of grey, but they're called tippler pigeons," Baba resumes.

"Oh, okay, I didn't know that. What's so special about them?"

"There are lots of things special about them. Firstly, they are very intelligent, just like you," he says to me, smiling.

I broaden my chest, just like I see Bhai doing when he feels proud about something he does and is complimented on it. I also manage to steal a glance towards Bhai, who makes a face at me—this time, quietly.

"Second, they have exceptional endurance."

"Umm…What does that mean?" I ask, confused. Baba has this habit of using really big words sometimes. They fly over my head before I can even pronounce them in my mind.

"It means they are tough; they may not look like it, but they are. They can fly for almost an entire day. Twenty hours or so."

"But they look so lazy. Just sitting in a line. So…idle. Like they have no worries," Bhai says.

"Yes, Zohaib, but we can't be so quick to judge, can we? You know these birds are so tough and intelligent that there are flying competitions they're entered into. People train them and then get prizes if their tippler wins."

"Sort of like a dog race, but for birds. And in the sky," I say smugly.

"Haha! Yes, exactly like that."

"I can't believe it, though. They look so peaceful. Like they could sit on those wires all day," says Bhai, deep in thought.

"Yes, *beta*—just remember, sometimes things are not what they seem; don't be fooled by the idle stance of the tippler pigeon. Always make it a point to discover. Look. Observe."

We are walking along Seaview, the air smells of salt and fish. Baba likes to take early morning walks along the beach to clear his head, he says. I tag along if I am awake. Sometimes, Bhai goes with him. I usually don't wake up this early on a Saturday morning.

36

He likes to take one child at a time for what he calls "quality time." Today, I guess, both of us wanted some "Baba time." The sun is not completely visible yet, but the sky is filling with colours telling us it will be here soon. I can see a lot of oranges and blues. Any minute, we should be able to see the semicircle of a bright yellow-orange ball rising. It's not cold, but it's not hot either. We are somewhere in the middle. I crane my neck back to where the pigeons are, still trying to imagine them racing.

"Can I go look for shells, Baba?" I ask excitedly.

"Not this time, *bachey*. I have to be in court early today."

My Baba is a businessman. I don't know what business he does exactly, but he has a huge office. He has lots of people working for him. They run a mill. I don't know what a mill is exactly either. Maybe I can ask him someday. He seems to be in a faraway mood today, so I just nod and slide my fingers through his. His palm is warm and rough. But I like holding it. We don't get much of a chance to speak at home. These walks are the only time I get with him. He takes Bhai with him for Friday prayers, and even for tennis sometimes, but I don't really like sports that much. Plus, Bhai says I'm a bad tennis player because I can't hold the racket right. He says Nono does it better than me, but, of course, Baba will not take Nono for tennis. I am his daughter, after all. Nono has a baba too, who she calls Abba. He lives in the village and sometimes comes to collect money from Masi. I don't like the look of him, but I've never told Nono that. He's always smoking or spitting, and Mama says it's bad manners. But I don't tell Nono that either. I don't think she would like to hear it.

The sun is up now. I imagine a smiley face inside its roundness, but it's too bright when I look directly at it. I close my eyes and try again. Baba squeezes my palm into his hand, and we keep walking quietly along the Seaview.

NADIA

Lahore, Pakistan

My life wasn't meant to turn out like this. I was going to stay in Okara, marry in Okara, have children, and then eventually be buried in Okara.

My amma started working for the Hashims just about the time my abba started beating her. We were a lot of children, and our parents never had enough money to feed all of us. Abba started smoking something. Something that was more expensive than the normal cigarette. To date, I don't know what exactly it was. The irony of escaping a *nashai* household, by marrying right into another one. They say you end up subconsciously choosing a man like your father. I wonder if that's what I did.

I must have been around four years old when it all started. It was the same pattern every night: Abba would come home late and instigate a fight with Amma over anything; there would follow shouting, screaming, and sometimes Amma crying. Abba would ask Amma for the little money she earned from all the cotton-picking she did in the farmlands. Abba used to work as a shepherd, till he lost track of all the sheep he was supposed to look after, having fallen asleep on the job. The *zamindar*, whom the sheep belonged to, had found Abba and kicked him between the legs to wake him up.

"Go inside," Amma said to me as soon as Abba came back from work one dreadful day.

I guess she could see from his eyes what I couldn't.

"But why? I'm not done collecting the rice from the floor," I said. Or was it beans I was gathering?

"Because I say so. Hush! Shoo!" she urged, pushing me behind her, despite my protests.

"You! It's your fault! You don't work hard enough. I have to hear shit from that swine, that piece of filth, because of you all!"

Amma must have realized that the blows were going to come down soon.

"Nadia, go. Go inside," she had pleaded when the first slap came. I dropped everything I had collected and hid behind the *charpoy*, perfectly visible.

"And you! What are you whimpering on about? What a curse you are, you little shit," he hollered.

I was so scared; I felt the warmth of urine trickle down my little legs. I still remember the smell, forever sealed in my mind as the stench of fear and humiliation.

Shortly after, Amma vowed to get me out of there. She had already spoken to her sister, who worked for someone in Karachi, doing their housework. She hadn't been planning to take me with her, but I was just four and Abba was uncontrollable. There was no way I could be left behind alone while she was away for work.

We took a tearful bus ride from my village to the main city of Okara. From there, a day-and-a-half train ride to Karachi. Amma was sad to leave my other siblings behind, but she couldn't take everyone. Abida was a few years older than me, Iqbal a little older than her, and Rubina, the eldest, was fifteen. Rubina was engaged to the son of my *mamu*, who was also going to give his daughter in marriage to Iqbal, in *wattasatta*, when the time came. Amma later told me that she had to raise money for her daughters' dowries herself, but I think she just wanted to get away from Abba. We were also leaving Gulshan behind. Gulshan, my cousin, my friend. The only friend I had known. Gulshan didn't have to worry about anything, though. Abba never hit her. Amma said it was because she was his dead sister's daughter, and that was the only ounce of decency Abba had left in him.

I remember packing myself a bag. It was a small *thaila*, one I had saved for when I stayed at my aunt's house. It was a plastic bag, but a big sturdy one. *Imtiaz Supermarket*, it read. My *khala*, Razia, brought a lot of crisps and biscuits in it for me when she came to visit us from Karachi a few months ago. Colourful small cakes, and big packets of chili and salt crisps. And she had brought Rio biscuits, with their signature dual-colour cream filling: blue and pink. Amma packed two frocks with tights, one pair of *chappal*, one hairband, one toothbrush and a packet of Rio for the train ride, while I gathered up all the pebbles Gulshan and I had been collecting for months. I also kept a *taweez* she had given me for safety on our travels and in our new life in the city. Teary eyed and out of breath, Amma had said, "I'll come back for you," to my brother and sisters.

I always think of my life as "before" and "after." Not that there was much "before." They say there is no way a four-year-old child could remember so much. But who knows how old I was? I often asked Amma, but she would tell me she didn't remember. I could have been four or five or six. In my suitcase of memories, I was just a young child.

The Hashims came from Punjab but had lived in Karachi all their lives. They looked like those English-speaking, upper-class types, and spoke even to their two-year-old daughter in English. They had a huge garden, with mulberry trees lined up near the alley that led to the servant quarters. The mynah birds sang all morning, the *chowkidaar* wore a uniform, and, for some time, it felt like I was in a movie. I made a friend—my first, after Gulshan. She was beautiful, my Misha. She had curly brown hair and brown eyes. Her nose was perfect, her face almost the shape of a heart, with that narrow chin. She was fierce and selfish and kind, all at the same time. She was sometimes a *titlee* and sometimes a wasp. She wanted the best for me and sometimes wanted the best for herself. She could never know what it was to be me, a lesser being: a person who wasn't born with privilege.

A sharp pain pierces my insides—for a moment, I'm startled by the intensity of this spasm. I've heard that trauma can take the form of an ache in the body. I breathe deeply, releasing the tension that comes to me whenever I think of her. My Misha. She was capricious, excited about the world that was promised to her. Sometimes she would drive us straight into trouble; at times, she would be at fault, but mostly that would not be her intention at all. I am everything I am today because of her. I am everything I am today, despite her.

*

I gather my reports and my bag and wait for Mubashir to come home. I have just returned from work and was hoping he would take me to Shadab *sahab*'s house on his bike. But, typical Mubashir, he said he had work to do and that he would be back by five p.m.—of course, his five p.m. could mean anything. I pace

41

around the modest room, back and forth. I try calling him, but he doesn't pick up. I check the time again. If I don't want to be late, I will just have to take a rickshaw. That's the thing about Mubashir: I can never rely on him.

I look around the room. The *charpoy* is unmade, with last night's mattress still strewn over it. There are several dirty cups on the counter, the residue of sweet tea attracting flies. Mubashir drinks *doodhpatti* and I'm pretty sure he even adds cheap *bhang* to it occasionally. And, by "occasionally," I mean any time he gets a chance to pinch my wallet for money. I feel the urge to rage-clean everything before leaving, but I'm short on time and need to get going.

Shadab *sahab* lives in Gulberg. It is at least twenty minutes from where I am, if I go through Mall Road. Twenty-five, if I take Lytton Road. This time of day, there will be a lot of traffic on Mall Road.

I walk along the gully near my house, the open drains releasing a terrible stench. All of this is a stark contrast to the pomp and glory of this city: the magnificent persona experienced by someone who is new to Lahore. The minarets of Shahi Qila, the enchantment of River Ravi, the splendour of the Badshahi Mosque—all bring about an aura of anticipation, a promise unfulfilled: a plea, highlighting the ravishing asymmetry of this celebrated city. I cover my face with my dupatta. The street is lined by repair shops, fruit carts, vendors selling local delicacies. My stomach growls and I remember I skipped lunch. I buy half a dozen bananas and pop one in my mouth right away. Rickshaw drivers usually spike up their rates in the evening. I wave my hand at one, signalling him to stop.

"*Bhai*, how much will you ask for, if you take me to Gulberg and back?"

"Do I have to stay there?" he asks, raising his thick eyebrows slightly. He looks me up and down, judging if I can afford such a luxury.

"Yes, but I won't pay you upfront. What if you run away? Who will find me a rickshaw at night?" I ask.

"But I will charge 350 rupees. Okay with you?"

"I'll pay 300, final," I assert. It's the end of the month and I am not left with much to spare. I pray silently that he agrees. I know 350 rupees for waiting for a passenger is actually exceptionally reasonable for the rickshaw drivers.

The air is warm and dry. The road we stand on is in disrepair, severely damaged in several places. He and I both know people walk further up the road to hail a rickshaw, to avoid these potholed rollercoaster rides. The road's condition improves as it goes along, but here, in my colony, the municipal authority ignores the complaints of its residents and the hazardous state of their roads. Who would come here to take pictures and organize repair, anyway?

He looks at me to protest, then seems to change his mind. Maybe he sees my desperation.

"Okay, *baji*. Today, I will listen to you. Maybe someday I will need you to honour my price."

"*Shukriya, bhai*," I say, adjusting my dupatta.

We reach Shadab *sahab*'s house at exactly six p.m. I've consumed three more bananas on the way. I put the remaining two in my bag. The rickshaw stops near the giant black gate.

"I'll be out in ten minutes. Please, *bhai*, don't leave."

"Don't worry, *baji*, I'm not going anywhere," he says, looking at the property.

I look around for a bell or buzzer to be let in but find none. I tap on the metal gate gently at first and then a little harder

43

with my knuckles. The doorman opens the gate and looks at me quizzically. I tell him I've come to see Shadab *sahab*. He looks me up and down then nods for me to follow him in. The garden is small but well maintained. There is a big coconut tree that's almost venturing outside the boundary wall. My head is light, and I feel a strange tingling at the back of my throat. The doorman leaves me at the entrance of the house where a maid is awaiting me.

She greets me and leads the way through the house. As we walk down the hallway, I notice the floral wallpaper and how it is peeling at the edges. We arrive at the lounge where she says I can sit and wait. She leaves and I realise just how quiet the house is, and that makes me a bit uneasy. There's no sign of his wife or children being home.

The lounge is a compact room, pleasing to the eyes. The sofa I sit on is beige, with printed cushions. I adjust myself so I have some back support. The maid returns with a tray and serves me water. I gulp it down within seconds, trying to quell my increasing anxiety. There is a large standing air-conditioning unit, but she doesn't turn it on for me.

Ten minutes later, Shadab *sahab* walks in. He is still dressed in his office clothes. He must have just returned from work. I take out the reports to show him the discrepancies.

"No need," he says, holding his hand up.

"B-but..." I stutter, confused.

"Come here, Nadia. I wanted to talk to you about something," he says, gesturing to the seat next to him.

I can smell his cologne from across the room. It is a mix of oud from his pilgrimage to the Holy Kaaba and some flowery scent combined. Shadab *sahab* is resting one hand on his lap and, with the other, he strokes his neatly trimmed beard.

"Sir, I think I will just leave the reports here," I say, placing the reports in the centre of the table and getting up to leave.

"No, no. I told you. Come here. You work too hard and worry too much." He gives me a smile, displaying his yellow stained teeth. "Today, I want to get to know you, Nadia."

Dread has slowly been gripping my tense body even before he utters these words. My name on his tongue feels like a defilement. This is going to be uncomfortable. How am I to protect myself without completely sabotaging my employment?

I look around the room, as if a solution to my dilemma might materialize. I can't afford to lose my job. At the same time, I am not ready to submit to this.

No, not again.

I need to think quickly. And wisely.

"Shadab *sahab*, Director *sahab* won't be happy if I go to him with a complaint, you know. Last month, Uzma was telling me she heard there have been too many complaints. Now, a respectable man like you should never have to worry about that. Here, you can have these, and let's just say this never happened."

I don't wait for him to respond. He is stunned by my directness, and I take the opportunity to head to the door. I run as soon as I slide it open, down the hallway to the main gate. My hands are trembling, my face covered in sweat. I don't look back. I'm almost sure Shadab *sahab* is not following me, but I can't be certain, and I dare not check. I reach the main gate and pull it with all my might.

"*Bhai*, quickly, quickly!" I shriek at the rickshaw driver.

"What happened? Why are you crying, *baji*?" he asks, running the engine.

"Just go. Please, *bhai*. Fast!"

45

I take a breath only when we've left Shadab *sahab*'s street. Wiping my face, I relax my shoulders. Deep breaths. I didn't realize I was sitting at the edge of the seat.

"What happened, *baji*?" the rickshaw driver asks, his tone notably softer.

"Nothing, *bhai*. This world. This world is not for the poor. We are here to entertain them. People who have been blessed with the wealth of *dunya* think it's okay to rob us of the only thing we poor have: our dignity. They think it's for sale."

"Don't say that. Our Lord sees and hears everything. Don't be sad. Good things will happen," he says, with a faith and conviction I envy.

I don't know what to say to him. I've been broken and put together so many times, I'm missing pieces of myself. And I'm waiting for good things to happen. I have been waiting for a lifetime.

We spend the rest of the journey in solemn silence. I pay the rickshaw driver and walk along the gully. I avoid the manholes, the iron covers stolen by heroin addicts. A raindrop lands on my face—the promise of relief from the sweltering heat of the day. I look up, defeated. If my Lord was here, life wouldn't hurt so much. If He was here, I wouldn't be taken advantage of. My eyes water, the moisture mixing with the rain. Where are you, my *Khuda*?

ZOHAIB

"Exhale, and, through the next inhale, transition into an upward-facing dog pose or cobra, whatever your practice calls you to today," says the long-limbed yoga instructor in a low, calming tone. Her accent sounds German, or is it French? I always get confused between the two; I do know the Germans have *khh* in everything.

Talha looks at me sideways in his perfect upward-facing dog. Suddenly, I'm hyper aware of the imperfection of my pose: how my thighs always touch the ground, I can never seem to keep them lifted. But, on cue, my mind interrupts my concentration, and I find myself switching between thoughts. Whitaker says, whenever I feel overwhelmed by multiple thoughts, I should focus on a single memory that relaxes me. Today, I begin thinking about kites.

I see in my mind's eye the red one flying, with the green lower half, sailing through the Karachi sky. I see Misha running gleefully towards it, following it everywhere. The roof is large and expansive. Our kite is not the only one flying. There are many others punctuating the clear blue sky with dashes of colour: blue, matching the colour of the ocean; yellow, like Mama's biryani; purple, like the butterflies on Misha's dress. It's windy, but the reel is sturdy in my hands. I roll, pull, release, tug. Release, pull. I let the kite sway. There is someone else there, besides Misha, and I'm speaking, but don't know to whom. The sheer strain of recollection is exhausting me. I can't, I don't want to think about it anymore.

"Take a deep breath in, hold it for a moment, and then exhale," the instructor says.

With the kites dashed from my thoughts, my mind wonders if I locked my apartment door this morning. What if something happens to Misha?

I notice the yoga instructor looking at me in a concerned manner. We have moved on to chair pose. My legs are hurting. I'm breathing hard.

I speed-walk out of the stuffy room. Outside, the wind hits my face like a slap. I've left my jacket inside. I don't want to go inside the room again. I hate yoga. What's the point, anyway?

"Dude, what happened?" Talha runs out after me, holding my blue puffer jacket. He knows I don't like yoga, but he also knows I don't like most things.

"I can't breathe in there. The k-k-kites. They're flying. I c-can't…" I say. I don't know where that memory has come from. I know it's an important one because it's hurting me. It's hurting my insides.

"Okay, okay. It's okay. We don't need to do it today," Talha says, his voice betraying the worry he's trying to conceal. Talha has seen my episodes before and always gives me time to recover from them. We have been friends long enough for him to know my rhythms; he knows when to slow down, when to pick up speed, when to draw close and when to make space. For all his encouraging me to try new activities, he's great at letting me escape them.

The truth is, I want to go back home, but how do I do that when I don't even know where home is anymore? Mama's, Baba's, or mine? Where do I go? My apartment is always dark, there is no one to embrace, no warm cup of coffee. Coffee is at the café. Is the café more my home? Or is it Dr. Whitaker's office, where I sit with my memories, where I reminisce about my visions of home: Mama, Baba, Misha, Nono? The laughter we shared, the joys, the innocence, the hopes and dreams. And the pain. All the pain, the loss. That happy picture shred to pieces and flung by fate to be scattered on the wind. What of this is real and what is drawn from the figments of my imagination? What is the past if not our memories, and what if we lose those memories? Do we lose our past too, as if it never happened?

There's a pain in my chest, and I'm struggling to breathe. There's an invisible weight bearing down on my body, as if the sky itself has slowly descended upon me. I have my head in my hands, and the pain has reached the corners of my eyes. I have succumbed to the pain and the flood of memories—my knees have given way. I want to scream, but I stay sitting quietly, gently rocking. It's so cold, I had forgotten my jacket. No, wait, Talha had it in his hands. Talha, can I hear his voice? Maybe I'll just freeze on this pavement, and it will all be over. I'll deserve it, for all that I did—what did I do? I'm hurt, I have hurt. I see them again: the kites are flying, red, purple, green. What if I let them go? I can feel a throbbing, shrieking pain. I deserve this. Let this consume me. Maybe, just maybe, the exhale may feel like forgiveness. Forgiveness is an exhale away; I need to release. Just let go. It's dark and cold. I close my eyes.

TALHA

Zohaib is my mate. He's the brother I never had, and I cannot bear to see him struggle like this. I only insisted he give yoga a chance because I knew he needed the physical activity, and I hoped it would help calm him. I can't believe it's backfired like this.

Zo and I have seen a lot of ups and downs. I grew up in Brent, with three sisters. My parents migrated to London after they married—my father an electrical engineer, my mother a teacher. They built a life and a home here for all of us. By the time I was born, the last of four children, they had already been away from the motherland for almost fifteen years. I knew little of my culture and relatives. Pakistan was just a green flag for me, hung nostalgically outside my parents' room. I'd never questioned who I was or where I came from, but in my teens the colour of my skin and the foreignness of my name seemed to erect an invisible barrier around me. White friends made jarring comments in passing, about curry and terrorism, and brown friends were few and far between. Those from within my parents' social circle

50

openly declared me a "coconut" for my lack of any cultural knowledge—no Urdu, no love of Bollywood, and no religiosity. No one could have guessed at the strife inside my head, because I astutely donned the cloak of the class quirk—not quite the clown, but just the oddball.

I met Zo in year ten. He was the shy kid with curly brown hair, lanky arms, always in a collared shirt. He arrived one day in our school as a full-board student from Pakistan. I liked him instantly, but he never seemed to notice me—or anyone, for that matter. Our friendship began the day he stood up for me against the bullies in our class. He stood by me when I felt lost, when I didn't know if I was in the right country, the right body, the right clothes. He put up a fight for me when people started picking on me. He stuck by me, defending me even when it gave him a bloody nose. I didn't have any idea of the magnitude of his own demons then.

When we finished our A-levels, it was time for him to move out of Farrukh Uncle's house. I knew what I wanted to do and where I wanted to apply. It's true, I wanted to study sports science at the University of Edinburgh. When I received the admission letter offering me a conditional place, I was buzzing. But Zohaib received letter after letter from universities announcing rejections. He finally received his conditional offer to study business at the University of West London. I could see him retreating into himself. He agonized over his future beyond boarding school and the routines and regimens he had around him. His parents were still not keen on him returning to Pakistan, and, with them being newly divorced themselves, the thought of him going back was unbearable for all of us who loved him. I decided to switch courses. I talked it over with my parents, who thought I was being naive and overly valiant, but they were also quite relieved that I'd gone for something a little more conventional for a change—they weren't too sure what sort of career sports science would lead to, apparently.

I admit, it wasn't all for Zo. I'd been feeling lost too, and he was my anchor. I know Zohaib's kindness, his generosity. The way his mouth curls up into a smile at the silliest of things, the way he gets worked up over little things like his alarm clock ringing twice. Late at night, when studying got too much for him, we would go for a walk down to Ealing Broadway, sometimes grab a cheeky Nando's. We would lose ourselves in dreams about our futures, imagining a world where we would be with the hottest girls on the most luxurious yachts and planes, the careers we would build, the cars we would drive. We would open a business together: he would open a health-food store and I would set up a sports department, or rehabilitation centre, right next door. We would be there for each other, always.

But things didn't exactly turn out that way. As uni drew to a close, Zo's anxieties about the future started to resurface, only this time he was obsessing over his sister, Misha. He would talk about the day the two of them were up on the roof in their Karachi home, and he'd become incoherent and dissolve into a sobbing mess on the floor. He got support from the student counselling services, and they helped him find a job within the university. He seemed to calm down at the realization that he wasn't going to be carted off on the first flight back to Pakistan, but, at around the same time, Misha came to stay with him. I never felt comfortable with that, but I didn't dare say anything—he was finally somewhat stable.

I managed to get myself a job in my final year of uni, assisting the yoga teacher and working in the recreational centre at the Third Space, Soho. Management have been considering setting up apprenticeships and have discussed enrolling me into a fitness programme. Maybe the dreams we had aren't so far beyond our reach?

I give Zohaib a few minutes to gather himself. We walk back to his apartment in silence.

MISHA

Karachi, Pakistan

"*Husha, busha!* And we all fall down!" says Nono, in a sing-song voice.

"Silly! It's 'A tissue, a tissue, we all fall down!'" I correct her. She can be so silly sometimes.

"No, it's not!" She makes a face.

"It is! Ask anyone!" I say, sticking my tongue out in annoyance.

She sticks her tongue out and scrunches her nose. She then cups her face and wiggles her fingers around it. She likes to go overboard sometimes.

"*Acha*, what does it mean, then? 'A tissue, a tissue'?" she asks. "Rhymes are supposed to make sense, Misha. 'We all fall down.' Why is it that we all fall down? Where do we fall down? Down in the garden, down in a dark well? *Where?*"

"You think too much. Down, just put your bum down. That's the way it is, dumdum."

"You're a bigger dumdum. You're a *da-dum!*" she says, her big *aha* moment.

"Shut up, you stupid. Let's just go see the rabbits in the garden," I say. I don't want to fight anymore.

We are on the veranda, where we usually hang out with Masi around, so she can keep an eye on us. It also has a clothesline that extends across the space. When Masi washes and hangs the laundry on a hot day, I like touching the cool wet clothes and sliding in the droplets of water dripping against the tiled floor. The veranda also has an open roof and a spiral staircase that leads directly into our storage area, but we are not allowed to go up there. I touch Bhai's trousers, hanging upside down. They're still wet, I notice with joy, but Masi is nowhere to be seen. I take Nono's hand and drag her off the veranda and into the hallway that leads to our big lounge. From there, we slide down the banister, as usual. There seems to be some commotion in the garden. It's usually quiet out there, unless we are playing, of course. But, today, a bunch of people are gathered, and they do not look like they're from around here. They look like they have come from some…village?

"What's happening?" I ask Akbar *chacha*, who's standing at the main gate.

"*Chotibaji*, these are Masi's relatives," he says, gesturing towards Nono, who suddenly seems smaller. She wipes her sweaty forehead with the back of her hand as she slowly recognises each of the people in the group.

"*Kaki!*" she shrieks, and runs towards a big woman with a dupatta draped around her face. I catch bits of their conversation in Punjabi, but can't quite figure out what's going on. All I can see is that Nono is meeting someone from her family after so long, but no one seems happy. In fact, they seem worried, upset. Nono is crying!

I rush to her side. I move forward to hug her. But she pushes me away. She looks at me and widens her eyes. It seems like she wants me to step aside, so I do. I feel the tears rushing out of my own eyes, but I don't even know why.

I turn around and run up the stairs to Mama's room, terrified. I am shivering.

"Mama! Mama!" I shout from outside her door.

The door is locked.

"Mama!" I know she's inside, probably in the shower.

She takes a few minutes to open the door.

"What? What happened?" she asks me, bewildered.

"Mama, Nono is crying and there are so many people. Something is wrong!"

"Okay, you need to calm down first. Masi! Bring her some water. Quickly!" Mama walks out of her room so Masi can hear her call.

Masi must have been ironing clothes downstairs, because she has her dupatta tied to her like a turban—something she only does while washing or ironing. She rushes to the refrigerator upstairs and presents me with a glass of cold water.

"*Baji*, here, *baji*." She has done as Mama said, but she doesn't seem herself. She puts a hand on her forehead, as if preparing for something bad to happen.

"Down—Nono is downstairs…" I tell her, pointing towards the gate.

Ring-a-ring o'roses,
A pocket full of posies.
A tissue, a tissue…

The three of us rush down the stairs, through the main door, and out into the passageway that leads to the garden. Masi

56

runs towards a shaking Nono and quickly embraces her. "What happened? What? Tell me!"

"She's...she's gone!" Nono says, now bursting into tears.

"Who? Who is gone? Nadia, tell me!" Masi shrieks, clutching her chest.

"Abida *bajjo*—someone took her! Kidnapped her!" Nono says, before her eyes roll behind her eyelids. She shakes a little and then collapses on the ground. I look wildly from Masi to Mama and feel a little dizzy myself.

...we all fall down!

NADIA

I have this recurring memory. I must've been young, because it's in the time of "before", when Amma and I still lived in Okara. Many people think of Okara more as a village, but the city itself is very developed. Our house was in Faridpur Sohag, a locality an hour's distance from the city. Amma had planned for us to move to the metropolis so Abida *bajjo* could attend school there—Resource Academia Okara Campus, an English-medium school that was celebrated as the best. She had married off our elder sister Rubina at a young age, but wanted a better life for her younger children.

My Abida *bajjo*. Her beauty was the kind you could just spend hours looking at. Like a princess, she was fair and had long brown hair. She had an upturned nose, giving her an air of pomp, as if she descended from rajas and maharanis; her eyes were hazel, and they sparkled when she talked. Everyone loved her. Everyone praised her. She was the best at everything, and all I wanted was to be exactly like her.

Back in those days, Amma would take us along with her to the potato fields. Some evenings, we would just wander around. Abida *bajjo* would help Amma, and I would…well, I don't actually remember what it was that I did. But I distinctly remember one time we were there, and I desperately needed to relieve myself. Hameed *chacha* was also roaming around nearby. Abida *bajjo* said she would accompany me because I had a habit of wandering off in the fields. I remember Hameed *chacha* being there, because he followed us around the bushes where I had decided to situate myself and I kept worrying he might see me. I had found an opening behind a thick bush and asked Abida *bajjo* to be on the lookout. I tried to squat, but my *shalwar* kept getting in the way. I heard a little commotion behind me, but I was just too busy trying to accomplish my seemingly easy task with great difficulty.

"Who is there? Abida *bajjo*?" I asked loudly, straining my ears so I could hear if there was a wild animal approaching.

No response.

"Bajjo?" I cried out again.

I cleaned up with whatever I found handy. Hurriedly, I pulled up my *shalwar* and looked around. There was not a soul in sight. No sign of Abida *bajjo* either. I roamed around the bushes for a while, and I remember the sun starting to set. She wouldn't just leave me, I thought to myself.

I finally found her sitting near an okan tree—the tree the city of Okara owes its name to. Its leaves are needle-like, and it is famous for its wood. She had her face cupped in her hands.

"Bajjo! I've been looking all over for you!"

"I…I'm sorry," she replied, a little disorientated. She looked stunning under the gold-streaked evening sky of Okara. Her eyes looked wild, her long thick lashes drenched in tears. Her dupatta had slumped off her head, her hair flying in the evening breeze. There was a red scratch on her cheek, bleeding slightly. I had never seen her like this before.

"Bajjo, are you okay?" I asked, frightened by the change in her appearance and behaviour.

She held me tight in response and walked me home in silence.

As we approached our gate, Abida *bajjo* suddenly knelt down so that she was eye-level with me. "Nado, listen to me," she said, holding my entire body's attention. "Never ever trust anyone, okay? Not your family, not your elders! Just don't let anyone come near you, ever!" she whispered urgently.

Her eyes darted to something far away. She held her dupatta tightly around her face—her eyes were wide and bloodshot. She was shivering.

"Bajjo, are you alright?" I asked her, confused at this break in her silence. Her face was unexpectedly flushed in the cool weather. She kept wiping her upper lip with the back of her hand, as if to remove some dirt.

I took her hand in mine and squeezed it hard. I wished I were her *bajjo*—her older protecting sister—but I didn't know how to be. I just knew something was terribly wrong. It was getting dark, and I was getting scared of the dogs barking in the distance, the grasshoppers chirping in the quiet.

Our house was inherited by my father after Dadajee's death. There was Hameed *chacha*'s share in it too, which I found out much later, when Abba passed away. It was a small dwelling, but a solid one, with walls made of concrete. Only one of the rooms didn't have a roof—the rest were fully covered. The rains had destroyed some of the rooms the year before, but the room

I shared with Abida *bajjo* somehow remained unaffected. Abba had told Amma a long time ago that he was saving to get the entire house painted and covered, but Amma wanted to sell it and move into town.

Abida *bajjo*'s eyes remained glassy, her clothes dirty. When Amma asked why, she just shrugged and said she fell. I knew she was lying.

Days passed, or perhaps it was weeks. Her wounds remained open, but unseen. She was a cemetery of grief, hope buried in her body forever. I used to stare at her during the day, her face betraying no emotion, her actions robotic. In the mornings, she would look out of the window, resting her chin on her palm. Through sleepy eyes, I would sneak a look at her, falling in and out of my slumber. She would help Amma clean and cook, and then accompany her to the fields. In the dark hours, she would do one activity obsessively—comb her hair for hours, or straighten her sheets, fixated on pressing the creases.

"Beautiful *bajjo*, princess *bajjo*," I said in a sing-song voice one night.

"*Chupkar*," she said to me angrily. Bajjo was never angry at me. "Beauty is a curse. And everybody wants to get a taste! I'm telling you, my *gurya*, if at any time in your life you feel something is not right—run! Run as fast as you can," she said, her voice desperate and her eyes darkened.

"Bajjo, why are you talking like this? Did Abba hit you? Did Bhai?"

She just stared at me without really looking, and went completely silent in the days to come. I tried to cheer her up, but then I became distracted by other things, as a child my age would.

I can't imagine what Abida *bajjo* felt, that night. I was too young to fully understand what had happened, to be able to help

61

her decipher her pain. Something broke in her and I wasn't able to comprehend the magnitude of it. The incident still jostles at my melancholy, for sorrow is a long-term project.

Abida's beauty would remain a curse for her. As for me, I had many other curses awaiting me.

ZOHAIB

I had to take time off work. I spent days in bed, but Mr. Osborne, my boss, was accommodating. He even organized flowers—lavender, marigolds and peonies—and a card signed by all the staff, to be sent to me at home. That was nice—why don't men receive flowers more often? Talha thinks I need a change of scenery, but I told him, "No, thank you." In the meantime, he took to playing the audiobook of *The Power of Now* at full blast in my apartment. I call it guerrilla spirituality. Once the fog of the first few days started to lift, I actually didn't mind it. Of course, it's reinforcing everything Talha says all the time: seize the moment, don't over-plan, and don't lose your chance of true happiness. Well, it doesn't say that exactly, but that's what I understood of it.

I'm back at work now, happy to make it out of the apartment. I look out from the window near my desk. The chair I am sitting on is uncomfortable, and the heating is far too high. It seems I shall either freeze in my apartment or boil at my workplace. Balance evades me. My desk is at the far end of the room. There is a window on my left—a large openable one, thankfully. Mr. Osborne gave me this spot because I told him I feel claustrophobic sometimes. He was quite nice about it. Despite his regular lamentations over how "flaky" the younger generations are, he is truly considerate. He gives me plenty of time to complete a task and is okay with me taking extended lunchbreaks. The work hours suit me. I haven't really made any friends. The receptionist, Mary, always smiles at me. And Cici—how do I even begin about Cici! I don't know why I lied about her in the first place—she has been nothing but kind to me.

An email alert draws me back to my computer. It's from Talha, who has been regularly sending me links to various holiday destinations. This time, the subject title reads, *The Inca Experience!* I reluctantly open it. A picture of Machu Picchu fills the screen, with miniature people dotted along the large mountain. The words, *The Inca Experience!* Slowly emerge on to the page.

I type "Inca Trail" into my browser and dozens of pictures show up of the green mountain. I search "visa requirements." It turns out British nationals don't need visas for Peru and, since both of us have valid British passports, we'd just need to book a tour guide. What am I thinking? It would be so stupid of me to leave Misha alone here. And selfish. No, I shouldn't even be considering it.

I quickly close the browser and open up Microsoft Word. I was supposed to update the attendance sheet and search for places for a school trip. I open my browser again. But I find myself searching online for all the trek companies in Peru. I learn you fly into Lima and from there take a short internal flight to Cusco. Cusco is supposed to be rich in heritage and beauty, but is also high in altitude, which causes altitude sickness in many visitors. Apparently, though, Mother Nature has a cure for that and there are local herbs available that help with acclimatizing.

All Star Peru, 5 Stars: All expenses covered—$650—Three Nights, Four Days—*Private Chef Included*

Action Treks Peru: $599—Four Nights, Five Days—*Private Guide*

Machu Picchu Adventures: Four Nights, Five days—*All meals, Private Chef and Porter included*

Just then, my phone buzzes with a text message. Talha.

Talha: *Hey, how's it going?*

Me: *All right, bro. Wats up?*

I glance around the room to see if anyone's looking—it's one thing slacking off on the computer when you can pretend you're busy working, it's quite another when you're obviously texting on your phone.

Talha: *Did you check out the link I sent you?*

Me: *No, I didn't*

Talha: *Dude*

I know he will be laughing. He knows I have.

Me: *LOL obvs I have. Happy?*

Talha: *And...?*

Me: *Can't leave Misha.*

Nothing. Then I see Talha is typing...

Talha: *She will be safe and happy with my parents, isn't it? You could leave her with them for a few days. It will be good.*

Really? No, I couldn't ask that of them, I think, but a part of me feels inclined to do so. For a second, I let myself get excited at the prospect of leaving London. I haven't left this city for so long and the thought of walking up a large green mountain, instead of through an urban jungle, suddenly doesn't seem like such a bad idea.

Talha: *Zo?*

Me: *Okay, let's do it.*

I stare into the phone, at those four words impulsively typed and sent off, and think about what I've done. Too late to delete—Talha already texted back with a multitude of emojis! What will Dr. Whitaker say? Will Misha be okay with me leaving her with Aunty and Uncle? My mind is instantly flooded with a million thoughts.

My immediate concern is money. I'll have to ask Baba for money if there isn't enough in my account. I know he will be fine bankrolling the trip if he thinks it's a good idea. On the one hand, he may be even more enthusiastic than I am. That will irritate me. His optimism will creep under my skin and gnaw at my core. On the other hand, he may put on a display of paternal angst, and worry I'm not well enough to make such a trip. And that will piss me right off. And he will try, as always, to probe. He'll ask too many questions about how I'm doing—enquire beyond what I want to share. He will put on an air of joy and try to talk father-to-son, as if there isn't a chasm between us.

I pull out my phone and tap on the Barclays app. I scroll to the balance, urging it to show me enough to save me the phone call.

£876.82

Urgh, that won't cover my travel expenses, and I know I will need some amount of money for immediate expenses after returning from the trip. I don't know what Baba will make of this trip. Will he be for or against it? Will he think it's good for me or argue that it's unsafe? Well, he's not in *my* head, is he? I need to do this. My life feels like it is slipping away. I've felt lost for so long now, left by my own parents to fend for myself. Mama hid in her room and Baba in his work. Me? I was so young then. Now, I'm just a guy who still has no clue about life. It is neither good nor possible to exist entirely alone. I pick up the phone and dial Baba's office number. This time, I call the shots.

MISHA

Karachi, Pakistan

Nono has been so sad since she found out about her sister. Her *bajjo* has been gone for more than three months now and there is no word from the kidnappers. Nono had to return to her village with Masi for a while, but she's back now, and quieter. She still plays with me, though sometimes she just shuts down completely. I try to be funny around her, but I guess I can't replace Abida *bajjo*. I only met her once—last year, when she came to our house along with her dad to pick up Nono and Masi for a short visit to their village. Her younger brother was also with her. I don't quite remember his name though.

We've planned a family trip to Dubai over the weekend, but I don't want to leave Nono behind like this, sad and alone. I have been wondering what to do, and today I think I finally found a solution to this problem.

"Mama! Mama! I have an idea. Let's take Nono with us to Dubai!" I say excitedly, barging into Mama's room like I've uncovered some brilliant scheme.

Bhai is busy doing his homework on Mama's desk, and she's dictating something boring to him. He is usually the first one to shoot down my ideas, but, miraculously, this one he seems to like.

"Yes, that's a good idea. But I don't really know how exactly we can make that happen," he says.

"Misha! You come up with truly crazy ideas. The girl doesn't even have a passport!" Mama exclaims.

"But we can buy her one, can't we?" I say, my tone hopeful.

"Silly! Passports can't be bought. You have to apply for them," says my know-it-all bhai.

"Poor girl must not even know her birthday!" says Mama. "Although, I suppose we could get her one."

"Really?" asks Bhai, seemingly intrigued.

"Yes—well, generally, you need a B-form from NADRA, the agency that issues identity papers when a baby is born. But, if Nono doesn't have one, that's okay. I can get someone to print a fake one for her," Mama says thoughtfully.

"A fake one?" My eyes widen in amazement.

"Isn't that, like, illegal?" Bhai asks now, raising his eyebrows.

"Well, not really. The poor girl will need an identity card and the only way to do it is to submit a fake B-form. And, *voilà*, Nono will be officially born, according to the laws of Pakistan!" Mama exclaims excitedly. "Does she know the date she was born?"

"We've never celebrated her birthday," Bhai says quietly.

That's true, I think. We've never celebrated Nono's birthday. I always have a party with friends and cousins, aunties and uncles, presents, food, and cake. Bhai goes out with his friends to celebrate his birthday.

"If we do take her, she could help out with cooking and laundry, instead of organizing a maid out there," Mama says,

68

almost to herself, rubbing her chin. I don't think much of it because I've had another bright idea!

I rush out of Mama's room and run towards the veranda, where Nono is doing her homework, and excitedly announce, "Let's get you a birthday!"

"What? What are you talking about?" says Nono sleepily. She must've dozed off against the wall she was sitting beside.

"Do you know how old you are? Or when the actual day was that you were born?" I ask eagerly.

"No…"

"So that means you can make up your own birthday!" I squeal, delighted with my intelligent plan.

"Well, there must be some birthday on my school form. Or maybe not. I don't know how your mama got me the admission," she says, uncertain.

"Sooo, what month would you like to choose?" I say, ignoring her concerns.

"Well, I like December because it's cold, but it's too cold in Okara. I like March because we have a spring festival at my school. Oh, oh, I know! August—because it's Pakistan's birthday! The fourteenth of August!" she says cheerfully.

"But then everyone will be celebrating *Pakistan's* birthday, not *yours*!" I say, knowingly. I almost sound as smart as Bhai.

"Oh, yes, you're right. I've got it! The thirteenth of August! And let's say this year will be my eleventh birthday! No, twelfth!" she says, her joy apparent.

"Hey, that's not fair! You can't be that old! You can't be four years older than me, or you'll just have to be Bhai's friend, not mine," I say, adamantly.

At that proclamation, she smiles shyly. I don't understand if she really plans to choose Bhai over me, but I let it slide. After all, she has smiled widely for the first time in days. I like a smiling Nono.

"The thirteenth of August, right before Pakistan's birthday!" she says, happily.

From this day on, we are going to celebrate Nono's birthday on the day she's selected for herself. Her personally chosen date of birth.

MASOOD HASHIM

Karachi, Pakistan

I put down the phone and wonder where it all went wrong. How does one define chaos? A state of utter confusion. Disorder. Maybe the infinity of space or formless matter. Like a volcanic eruption in the middle of the ocean—the unforgiving, pitiless sky dropping down to its knees. A lack of intentional design.

I feel like that every day of my life. But that one incident squeezed the breath out of us ordinary beings, making us surrender to our devastating fate. Our existence has been shattered into diminished pieces of nothingness ever since. I lost all that mattered to me, all that I valued.

Plato says, "There are two things a person should never be angry at: what they can help and what they cannot." Looks like he doesn't leave us much choice. So, what does one do if one is angry all the time?

Faiza was the one who kept me balanced. *Don't overthink it*, she would say. *Take a deep breath and think, How significant will this really be in a year?* She always made me see the logic of things—the bigger picture. She calmed me down. Why did you leave me, Faiza, when I needed you the most?

Do we really suffer from ourselves or from each other? Do we really destroy our *nafs*? Is hell a homecoming? Are the ones still alive worth living for?

When I think about Zohaib, my gut tells me to keep him close to me. A father will always need his son and vice versa. But what did I do instead? When the going got tough, I let go of him. I thought distance would protect my son, so I kept him far away from his home, but spent every last rupee I had on him. My heart was hollowed out, my mind redundant, and Faiza was absent. She had abandoned herself to tumble deep into her own abyss. *Why didn't you tell me to hold on, Faiza? Why did you choose yourself just then?* Without my anchor, I was left stranded in my chaos. What was I to do?

I visited Zohaib two years ago, and only once before that. Twice in over a decade. Am I that selfish? I am astounded at myself. But each visit was excruciating, for us both. Zohaib had fewer and fewer words for me, and I struggled to spend time with him. His eyes seem frozen in the shock of that fateful day. They're still haunted by what they witnessed, and I cannot look at them without feeling like they will pull me in and under. Yes, I suppose I am that selfish. Why do I want to save myself the pain? Did he deserve to be abandoned like this? Every breath I take hurts me— smiling has become a distant memory. I have become a veteran of sleepless nights. Oh, but when sleep does come, my dreams take me to only one place: the Karachi seashore, where I walk hand in hand with my two children. I am whole. But, when I awake, I am left with the sounds of those waves still echoing in my ears, and I wonder, will the tide ever turn in favour of my family?

The walls of my empty house scream their silence as I walk along their length. The furniture is kept pristine by the house staff; every piece was lovingly picked out by Faiza in the belief that we had an eternity to spend together with it. Now, it leers at me when I brush past it. I could just move out, so the memories don't haunt me every minute of my existence, but there's a penance I need to pay, and this seems to be a start.

Where is my Lord when I need Him the most? My Lord— my guidance, my light? Where am I going to go from here? Why is the *nafs* causing me misery and not providing me with the tools to deal with this continuous pain? Where is my *wujud*, my spirit? My *Rabb*, can You guide me?

MISHA

Bhai and Nono have started spending a lot of time together. I'm feeling a bit left out, since they are treating me like I'm an outside joke. You know how they have *inside* jokes? Well, I don't really *get* theirs. Nono has started acting like she's twelve, like Bhai. They even share stationery. Bhai would *never* even let me borrow an eraser, but, for Nono, he emptied his entire pencil case! *Hmph!*

Maybe they are each other's true love. But Mama says you must not look for it too early, like right now. She says we are Muslims, and we need to find true love when we turn twenty years old and not a day before that. Then, we're supposed to marry our true love and have babies. But Nono and Bhai are jumping the gun—they're nowhere near twenty. I was hoping to take Nono to Dubai, but now we're not even going because Baba has a meeting he cannot miss and Mama doesn't want to go without him. Another one of my schemes gone down the drain.

Just as I am having these very important thoughts, Mama calls out to me, "Misha! Get ready! We're supposed to go for dinner at Zaheer Uncle's house. Oh, look at you, now—you have

74

chocolate smeared all over your face! Go wash up, quickly!" she says, rubbing something off my upper lip. Must be from the Nutella sandwich I just gobbled up.

"Faiza, which tie? Green or black?" Baba calls out from in front of the mirror in their room.

"Do you need a tie? How important is this dinner?" Mama asks him.

"Well, it's an alumni dinner. I will be rubbing shoulders with the city's elite," he says.

"I think the shirt is formal enough. The tie would just be trying too hard," she replies.

I quickly go to my washroom and splash water on my face. Some water gets onto my shirt. I'm glad I haven't changed my clothes yet, otherwise Mama would get angry at my wet clothes and chocolatey face.

"Where are you guys going?" asks Nono, standing at my bedroom door, which is full of stickers and glitter paper that I cut out and carefully put up as decorations. She scratches at one of the larger stickers, her eyes darting between me and the door.

I'm upset with her for leaving me out and choosing Bhai as her friend over me. I know I can't be angry for too long, but right now I feel like leaving *her* out. I can be like that too, you know.

"We're going to Zaheer Uncle's house. I have a friend there too: Hadia, their daughter. She has the best slime collection, by the way. Oh, and she also gives me imported M&M's every time I go to their house," I boast.

"I've had imported M&M's before. My cousin in Dubai brings it for me all the time," she blatantly lies. I know she has no cousin in Dubai.

"Well, they can't be as fresh and crispy as Hadia's. She also has the softest slime—it's called *putty*," I say, knowingly.

"Potty?" she smirks.

She is making me a little madder, now. I want to yell, *Of course it's not potty, you dodo*, but I just press my lips together and let it slide. I don't want to say anything to her that will make me angrier. She acts better than me, but I *know* more, okay.

"Anyway, I have so much work to do for my art project in school. My art teacher is just so cool. She told us to make musical instruments out of toilet rolls, tissue boxes…" Her voice trails off.

She knows I hate my art teacher. I grunt under my breath.

"Well, go do your art project, then. You're not invited, anyway," I say, spitefully.

"Well, I don't want to go, *anyway*," she retorts. With that, she leaves the room, leaving the door open.

She seems to be becoming meaner every day and I don't know if it's something to do with me or her, but it hurts. I feel confused and sad and angry, all at the same time. I shut the door and take out my fanciest dress to wear to the dinner. I even brush my hair without Mama pestering me about it. I take out a brand-new pot of slime I had bought for Nono and put a smiley-face sticker on its lid to gift it to Hadia. *I have other friends too, you know?* I think to myself before walking out of my room.

TALHA

London, UK

I cannot believe my plan has worked! Zo has agreed to go to Peru with me! I don't have anything to worry about, except to make sure my parents go through with the arrangement I have offered Zo for Misha. When it's just me and Zo, I can handle him. My parents, though still a little discomfited by Zo's situation, are also willing to help. They know him and they love him. Over the years, Zo has spent countless days with us and has been one of Mum's favourite bellies to fill with her array of dishes. They know the truth about Misha as much as I do, but this will be the first time they will enter into this predicament with her so fully. I've explained to them how important it is for Zo to get away—he seems to be on a downward spiral. To their credit, they have set aside their own misgivings to help the boy they've welcomed so wholly into their lives, who did himself support me at such a crucial time in my teens too.

For our trip, I have enough cash saved, and we'll book a hostel anyway, not those boutique Cusco hotels. In terms of the trek itself, I've already searched for the ones with larger groups so it's more economical per person.

I take the Tube from Brent Cross to Edgware Road to get to Zo's. There is hardly any space to sit, but it's a short ride, so I don't mind standing. Once out of the station, Zo's apartment is a ten-minute walk. I go up to the porch and press the buzzer.

"Yeah?" Zohaib says through the speaker.

"It's me," I say, confident that he recognises my voice.

The buzzer sounds and the iron door releases to let me in.

I press the button for the sixth floor in the elevator. The door closes noiselessly. When the elevator door opens, I walk over to the door of Zo's apartment, which is already ajar for me.

"Hey," he says.

"Hey," I say back.

"So, we're doing this, yeah?"

"Yes, we are," I confirm.

"Well, you still have to ask your parents…" he says tentatively. "She's sleeping, now." He gestures towards the bedroom.

"That's not a problem. I've already spoken to them, and they are happy to have Misha." I smile reassuringly.

I sit on the olive-green sofa, and he brings me a Sprite. I don't say anything about our plan yet. There will be time to figure out exactly what flights to take and when, what to pack, his doctor, my job, hotels, transfers, Misha. But, right now, I sit silently next to him, sipping my Sprite, while he sips on his cola, and revel in the knowledge and contentment of spending time with one another.

NADIA

The ceiling fan gurgles before finally coming to a grinding stop. I open one eye and look up from under my sheet to check what's happened. Mubashir lies soundless on his *charpoy*.

"Mubashir! Wake up! Check if the electricity is out or if it is just the fan." I can't even open my eyes properly.

His *charpoy* is close enough, so I stick my leg out and kick it.

"What? What?" He gets up, dumbfounded.

The room is stuffy. There is only one window that opens towards the back of the gully, making the ventilation in the summer particularly poor. My hair is already sticky from the sweat that's gathered on my scalp. A mosquito buzzes near me, and I slap my ear hard.

"Check the fan."

He turns the switch on and off. Nothing. He turns on the other switch and the room is suddenly flooded with light.

"Turn it off! I'm sleeping!" I shriek.

"You told me to check, so I'm checking!" A second later, he adds, "The fan is gone." There is not a hint of concern in his voice.

I swear a little under my breath. It seems there is a different unexpected expense lying in wait for me every day. Yesterday, it was the tap in our miserable kitchen. Today, it is the fan. Even the smallest pedestal fan costs four or five thousand rupees, these days. Sometimes, I think of getting a part-time job as a maid to deal with these piling expenses.

But, just as I start to convince myself to do so, my mother's assured voice rings in my ears: *You are never going to be anyone's masi, Nadia. You have what I couldn't ever get for myself.* My heart sinks, thinking about her.

Amma lost a son in Karachi's urban warfare in the late nineties. He was involved with the opposing party, calling strikes, burning tyres. Oh, Iqbal—you were just sixteen. She lost a daughter—albeit for a few months—to kidnappers, and kept wondering her entire life what they had done to her sweet Abida during that time. Abida always pretended that nothing had happened to her during her kidnap ordeal—that she had merely been held against her will, that the kidnappers hadn't known what to do with her when they realized her family was too poor to pay a ransom. But I could hear her screams in the middle of the night. I witnessed her nightly hauntings well into adulthood. I'm sure Amma did, too.

A few years after Amma and I went to Karachi, we heard Abba had passed away. People said he had killed himself, which sounds more sudden and tragic than it was, as I'm sure it was a slow and deliberate march towards death, due to all the drug abuse. His funeral was silent and simple. I remember very little of him. Amma is in a better place, now. Or at least that's what I hope for—this world was not kind to her.

I'm snapped out of my thoughts by a hand on my shoulder. It's Mubashir. My back towards him, I shrug him off. I don't like him touching me anymore. I don't love him. I'm not sure I ever did.

"What?" he asks. Despite our distance, when he is sober, he can still sense me falling into the abyss of my own heart, chasing old memories. Instead of softening me, though, it unleashes something.

"I want to leave you. I want a divorce. I can't do this anymore." There isn't a single ounce of feeling left for him in my heart.

"What? What are you talking about, *meri jaan*?" He's bolted upright. "I can't live without you, I can't…" His voice trails off. He's dumbstruck.

"Leave tomorrow. Pack your *nasha* and leave. Please."

"Where will I go? What's wrong? Did something happen?" He begins rubbing my back.

I turn around to face him. "Yes, something is wrong. You are. You are always out of it, and when you're not passed out, deep in intoxication, you're out in search of your next hit. My boss tried to take advantage of me the other day. You weren't there because you were off—God knows where—buying your next supply of drugs, no doubt. I have been paying for everything in this house, including your *nasha*! Get out now, Mubashir. Just get out of my house!" My rage is animal-like. Something wild and ferocious in me has awoken, and I don't try to control it.

"Baby doll, you're just tired and the heat has made you irritable. I won't do *nasha*, I promise! I'll get a job, tomorrow, *pakka*."

"You said that last month, and the month before that. Hell, you've been saying it for the past three years. You know what? I can handle the Shadab *sahabs* of the world. I'll fix the fan and pay for the electricity and rickshaw drivers, and you can get the hell out of here and lie on someone else's *charpoy*!" I say, sitting upright too, now.

I don't care if the neighbours hear us. I don't want to live like this anymore. I'm better than this.

"*Jaanu...*" he tries once more.

"Out—tomorrow," I say curtly. I quickly wipe the tears off my cheeks that have escaped my eyes in anger.

Mubashir looks at me. I remember the first time I met him, behind my college cafeteria. He didn't study at my college, but he had friends who did. He had dropped his studies after matric, but I didn't know that then. He was perfectly charming and attentive. He gave me more than I could imagine—he became my personal Shah Rukh Khan. He routinely bought me red roses—my favourite. He read my hand, claimed he knew palmistry. He asked me to marry him within months of us meeting. At the time, it felt so romantic, fresh, and exciting. Now, I look back with the hardened eyes of adult cynicism and find only clichés and a cheap imitation of love.

Perhaps I am being unfair. I didn't know much about Mubashir when I said yes. But I was living in a hostel, and most of my family was either dead or absent. I didn't feel I had much to lose, and I was all too keen for an escape route. As a young woman, you are taught that your worth is recognised by how many suitors you have. Someone to provide for you. At the time, I needed to depend on someone. I had been a little broken after the incident at the Hashims—the only home I'd known for many years of my life—and the case that was registered against me. There were days I felt like I didn't deserve to live. My past haunts me still. Mubashir was a temporary relief, a welcome distraction. I would've lost the case too, but the Hashims cancelled the charges against me at the last moment. Some late epiphany after the initial allegations. I had done nothing wrong. *Nothing? Really?* I hear myself ask. No. I was just a child.

ZOHAIB

Talha managed all the logistics to get us here. I felt a little spoilt and tried to help, but he was adamant he would manage it. All I had to do was pack, and sort Misha out. I spoke to Misha and asked her if she'd be okay without me, and she happily agreed. I was pleasantly surprised and yet it felt right that she would be ready to let me go now. Misha and I went to Aunty and Uncle's the night before my flight. In the morning, Talha and I thought we would leave everyone still asleep and quietly creep out at dawn, but Aunty was down before us and had cooked us a delicious breakfast of paratha and eggs before the taxi arrived to take us to the airport.

Talha and I took the flight from Gatwick to Lima, Peru, via Madrid. We flew with LATAM—a safe choice, since the layover in Madrid was only three hours. The flight attendant found Talha charming and kept flirting with him. I just enjoyed the interaction from a distance and kept my headphones on. I watched *The Room*, which would've been cool to watch on the big screen, and then followed it up with *Andaz Apna Apna*, downloaded on my iPad, taking me back to when I first watched it with my cousins, at the Alhamra house, on our ancient VCR player.

Talha and I have finally reached Cusco after almost a full day of travel. It's cold here and—just as the Internet warned—the altitude has made me feel light-headed. We were meant to stay here for at least two days, but it would have required Talha to take too much time off work, so we decided to spend only one night at the hostel we found on Booking.com. I didn't want to push Talha to book something fancy, because I know he's on a limited budget—we even travelled economy. We'll start early tomorrow: at six a.m., a van will come and pick us up from our accommodation.

"Do we h-h-have everything for the trek, mate?" I ask Talha, suddenly anxious about being in the middle of nowhere for three nights. "I've heard it's-it's very c-cold." I usually don't stutter this much, but I can't help it right now. I wish I'd packed Dr. Whitaker with me, too.

"Bruv, we're all set. Don't worry. We just need to rent a pair of walking sticks for you, and maybe we can get you some more thermals, if you're worried about the cold. The sleeping bags are being rented from the trek company. I've got everything under control," he assures me.

Of course, Talha has everything organized. I look at him and see him in focus. Talha is a good-looking guy. He's six foot one, at least two inches taller than me. He has bleach-blond hair, with roots revealing his dark brown mane, tamed by the half-bottle of gel in it. He's broad-shouldered and muscular—the perfect physique to endure a trek like the one we're about to go on. Me? I'm lanky—okay to look at, I guess. My hair is curly and brown; there's perpetual stubble on my chin, since I'm too lazy to shave frequently enough. I have hardly worked out in months, except that horrendous yoga class. I am not ready for this trek. I don't know why I agreed to this.

Oblivious to my weakening resolve, Talha continues to excitedly relay the itinerary for the next few days. "In the welcome email, I discovered we have a meditation guru in the group. He does some sort of intuitive therapy—that might be good for you, I'm telling you. Keep your muscle relaxants with you, but don't overdo it. We'll be on a schedule. You can't get left behind," he says carefully. He is balancing the tightrope well, keeping me prepared, but not letting me panic.

We leave the hostel and start walking towards the main square. Cusco is small. The streets are cobbled, and the sky is full of candyfloss clouds. It's mostly a tourist town. Many people avoid the trek and take the train directly to Machu Picchu. When I was young, it was my dream to be a mountain trekker. I was quick on my feet and played cricket on the street. A *natural athlete*, Baba would call me. Now, I can't concentrate on anything, and the thought of physical exertion overwhelms me. What was I thinking when I said yes to this? It seemed such a good idea, in the safety and familiarity of London, to go on an adventure. I'm worried about Misha too—she seemed okay with the idea, when I told her about it. Like she didn't care if I was there or not. But I know she needs me. She will always need me.

There are souvenir shops, pizza shops, and clothing shops mostly displaying their special Peruvian sweaters. I stop at one and examine a patterned turtleneck.

"How much?" I ask the shopkeeper. The locals here have almost the same skin shade as me, but I noticed even some of the young ones have wrinkles around their eyes. I wonder at this. What have they seen that leaves these cracks around their eyes so young? Can everyone see these lines around their eyes? I imagine

85

a world where our life experiences leave different markings on the body and only those with the same markings can see them on others. Maybe I have the same cracks in the skin around my eyes, a mark of something seen too young.

"Fifty soles," he replies eagerly.

"Huh? Nah, that's too much. Thirty soles," I say, countering the offer, and looking at Talha for approval. He rolls his eyes jovially.

"Final—forty," the shopkeeper replies, now pretending to be uninterested.

I fish thirty-five soles out of my wallet. He takes the money from me and starts counting it. When he realizes it's thirty-five, he scoffs and shakes his head. He puts the money in his pocket and hands me the sweater in a plastic bag. Another thing Peruvians and Pakistanis have in common: the art and theatre of haggling.

"No, thank you. Please don't use plastic bags," I say to him, taking the sweater without the bag. I think of wearing it on top of my long-sleeved shirt, but decide against it; it's afternoon and not very cold yet.

We walk out of the shop, and I spot a comfortingly familiar sight: Colonel Sanders, smiling at me from across the street.

"Can we grab a KFC before we head to the thermal shop? I'm starving!" I say to Talha.

"Sure. This place is just awesome, isn't it? So glad you came out," he says, patting me on the back.

We grab a couple of Zinger burger meals and continue exploring the town for another hour or so. The shop signs announce cafés and massage parlours. There's a herbal shop that catches my eye. It's getting dark and we still need the thermals, but I take Talha's arm and pull him towards the shop, remembering something about local herbs that help with altitude sickness.

86

"This looks interesting," I say.

The shop is lined from wall to wall with all sorts of things: socks, gems, herbs, posters advertising local services, necklaces, rings.

"Hi! What treatments do you offer?" I ask the old man standing behind the counter. With my stomach sated, I'm in a better mood to enjoy this trip.

"We offer reiki healing, chakra massage, ayurvastra, stone healing…" His voice trails off as he looks deep into my eyes.

I avert my gaze to look around the shop more attentively. There are jars of herbs lined up on the counters: maca red, maca black, annatto powder, chilli verde salt, and *Bixa Orellana* are a few labels I catch. The shop is quaint—there is a small fan placed on the counter, with several trays displaying lighters, chewing gum, penknives, and fridge magnets. There is another Peruvian man in the shop, assisting a customer—a woman with red hair. The shop has an eerie feel to it; smoke comes out of a genie lamp in the corner, filling the room with a hazy cloud. There is a rate list for the services they provide, and in front of more than one it states, *Upon request.*

"Don't you need a shaman for that?" I say pointing to ayurvasta rates.

"Yes, yes. You do. There are many kinds of healing. I see your soul is searching. You have pain. You need to let go of your past." He smiles at me. One of his canines is missing.

"I—I don't know what you're talking about," I say, the smile on my face fading.

"You don't need to run away from pain. You must embrace it. Peru has the highest energy forms situated in its centre. Cusco is where the grieved come. You have come to a place of healing. You've come to the right place. You will find peace here," he goes on.

I'm rattled, but also wondering if this is part of a performance he puts on for tourists. Everyone has some grief they carry, and who doesn't want peace? But I'm uneasy and I want to get away from him.

"There is a little girl..." he starts.

No. I turn on my heels, my eyes seeking Talha.

"Talha, let's get out of here." I don't want to hear what the shopkeeper might say next.

"In your journey, you will lose her, but you will get a second chance at doing right. Cusco will help you..." he calls after me.

I rush out of the shop with Talha behind me. It's freezing out here, but I am sweating. Talha looks concerned, but says nothing.

I'm confused and a little shaken by the interaction. Every cell of my body is buzzing. Dread and euphoria permeate the air in equal measure. I can feel it.

What *is* this place?

MISHA

Karachi, Pakistan

"Misha! Misha! Wake up, wake up!" Nono whispers in my ear.

It's maybe a Saturday, but I don't know for sure because I'm still half dreaming and not fully awake.

"Come *onnn*! Wake up!" she repeats urgently.

"What is it? Let me sleep. Go away!" I moan, turning in my bed. We are still not back to being friends, but I am also very sleepy. I can't imagine anything could be so urgent that she has to be so annoying this early in the morning.

"Misha! Flapper and Jacko are dead. I just saw them, limp on the ground. Come quickly, *na*!" she says, not waiting for me to respond. She grabs my hand and pulls me up. We both rush down the staircase, not bothering to slide down the banister this time. No time for that.

The main door is locked, and we can't reach the top lock. We go through the kitchen door at the back and run up to the garden where the rabbit hutch is. The two rabbits are flat on their backs and the third one is curled up in a corner. All three seem frozen, as if a witch has cast an evil spell. Tears fill up my eyes.

The ones on their backs are definitely Jacko and Flapper. I can tell because Flapper has a black spot surrounding one of his eyes, like a pirate's eye patch, and Jacko has black spots all over his back and belly. Sprinkle is completely white—she's the one curled up in the corner. When Baba brought the three rabbits home for us, we decided that Sprinkle was a girl and that Jacko and Flapper were boys, but the truth is we don't really know how to tell with rabbits. I do know, though, that the private parts are a little bit different for boys and girls. But I can't really talk about private parts because Mama says it's something you aren't supposed to talk about.

I know that Jacko and Flapper have been suffering from a disease, but I'm scared of what I see. Their behinds are completely black. It looks like a black fungus growing out of their bottoms. We had been warned by our vet. He told us about some disease that rabbits get, and when we went for their regular check-up, we were warned they wouldn't survive for long. It's a miracle that Sprinkle's behind is completely spot-free. She seems to be either acting like she's dead or is actually dead along with her two brothers.

"Are they dead or sleeping?" I scrunch my eyebrows, worried.

"Well, in that position, they look dead to me," Nono says, looking a bit calmer, now that she's delivered the news to me.

"Look! Sprinkle is moving! Oh, oh! She just opened one eye!" I exclaim, suddenly hopeful.

"Sprinkle! Sprinkle!" Nono says.

"Sprinkle! Come, buddy! You're alive! You're alive!" I jump for joy, ecstatic to see that it isn't all doom and gloom.

Sprinkle extends her leg lazily. Her ears perk up and she sniffs the air a bit. I reach out into the hutch to pet her, but accidently hit my elbow on Jacko's belly.

"Oh! I'm so sorry, Jacko!" I'm not sure how to speak to a dead rabbit. Is there a way to speak to rabbits that have passed away?

I pick up Sprinkle and she gives my sleeve a tug. I smile at her, feeling happy and sad at the same time. I know it's going to be hard for her now. When we first got the rabbits, they told us Jacko and Flapper came as a pair, and Sprinkle had lost her partner at the Empress Market, where she was first bought by the supplier. But they had quickly learned to be around each other. They would all run together, share their food, dig holes in the garden together. They had just become a gang of three. And now Sprinkle is by herself again.

It's a bit unfair, if you ask me. Although I'm happy that I still have her, it's going to be a tough and lonely life for Sprinkle. I could ask Mama to get me more rabbits, but I doubt that she will. She told me strictly that they were my responsibility. Yes, Shah Zaman gave them food and all, but their well-being was my duty and I have failed. I've failed them so badly.

"I think we should plan a funeral for them. Or a memorial. What do you say?" I ask Nono.

"Where will we bury them? Who will we call? They have no family," Nono states in despair.

"Well, it will be you, me, Sprinkle, and maybe Bhai. He can also say a little prayer," I suggest, stroking Sprinkle's ear. She struggles to get out of my grip, finally jumping onto the grass. "She's upset with me. See, she doesn't want anything to do with me anymore because I failed her brothers!" With this, I burst into tears—big, uncontrollable tears.

Nono wraps her arm around my shoulders in an awkward hug. She looks sad, too.

"It's okay. Every living being dies one day," she says. Suddenly, she seems so much older than me.

91

I know her father passed away a few months ago, which is why she went to her village. I know she has had a tougher life than me, but I'm amazed at how calmly she's taking it all. I'm feeling this loss much more than she is.

"*Chalo*, let's go to Shah Zaman *chacha* and ask him to help us bury them. Actually, can you tell Zohaib to call him? The kitchen is very hot. My face burns up every time I'm in there," she says, blinking her eyes rapidly.

I notice she has started calling Bhai by his name. But, in my sadness, I let it go. I think Jacko and Flapper deserve a proper funeral. And I will make sure they receive one.

NADIA

Mubashir has moved into his friend's house, but his stuff is still lying around. I didn't expect the rage that rose within me that night, but once it unleashed itself, like a storm, it left both an upheaval and a clearing in its wake. Maybe it was the fan, or Mubashir's incessant *nasha*, or just his general inability to do anything at all for me. I felt ambushed from every direction. I felt like prey as I walked the streets, and found no refuge in my work, nor home, and Mubashir would be carrying on without a care in the world. Isn't the husband supposed to be taking care of the wife's well-being in every way possible? Wasn't he supposed to be my protector? Isn't that what they love to tell wives? Or is it only when she does something supposedly objectionable that a man suddenly becomes aware of his wife's existence, only to burn, stab, or shoot her?

But I've had enough of him and his ways. In fact, I've just had enough of men.

What happened with Shadab *sahab* shook me. I haven't been able to concentrate on work for days now. I've been calling in sick and, the morning after I kicked Mubashir out, I called Khursheed *sahab* and told him I was still unwell.

I take out a saucepan from under my kitchen counter. The counter is stained and decrepit—the basin drain is just an open hole. Then there's the water issue: when the kitchen tap is running, the bathroom shower stops; when the shower is on, the kitchen tap goes dry. I pour water from the tap into the saucepan, thankful there is no one in the shower—my first win of the single life—and put it on the cooker to boil. Today, I'm going to put everything in order. I'll clean my quarter out, sell anything that I don't need, and make a plan to move out in three months.

When we first got this place, I thought it was only going to be temporary, but we've been living here for over five years. Every month, half of my salary goes to the landlord. He covers the gas, and we cover the electricity. Add to that the cost of food and transport, and I've pretty much spent everything I've earned since I started this job. For the first year or so, Mubashir would pick me up and drop me off on his bike, and that would save some of my money. But then he missed one day, and then another, and another—sleeping in, smoking up. Soon after that, I started noticing cash would go missing.

Every two years, I got a small raise from Khursheed *sahab*—so, twice, now. Each time, I planned to save the money to move out to a better place, but, each time, Mubashir would strike first. I didn't say anything, in the beginning; I didn't think it could be him. But, when there was no other culprit to be found, I remained silent. I had been taught to keep my husband's *purdah*, to stay quiet, not make apparent his flaws, not even to him. A man's ego mustn't be offended; it must be protected at all costs. I hoped he would see the error of his ways. I thought my generosity would win him back, or that his masculinity would be ashamed that his wife worked while he squandered away her money on such awful vices. I should've told him to stop. I should've asked him why he was wasting his life away. I just didn't. And now I just feel sick.

When I was younger and I visited Okara, I would see my family members always fighting. Fighting for money, cursing each other, cursing *wattasatta*, cursing life, even hitting each other. It was all very complicated, back home. When I tried explaining the dynamics to Misha once, right after Abida *bajjo* was kidnapped, she stared at me with her eyes wide, unable to comprehend the complexities and harshness of our relationships. Abba beating up Amma, Amma beating up Iqbal for being involved with the wrong people, Gulshan crying, Abida crying, Iqbal throwing up. Her life of privilege always kept her from fully seeing or understanding who I was and where I came from. She thought we were friends, but I ate in the kitchen while she ate at the dining table. I only got a passport because they had intended to save on hiring help on their trip to Dubai. I was relieved when it got cancelled at the last minute. Yes, they sent me to school, but that was less to do with any care for me and more to appease their own souls, and of course to mention it in passing to their friends. Aunty Faiza would wax lyrical with her kitty party friends about how important it was to give "a poor cleaner's daughter" a "fair chance at life," and they would all smile and nod with self-satisfaction as I refilled their porcelain cups, not noticing that I'd had to take the day off school so they could all be served their tea that day.

The water comes to a boil, and I put a spoonful of tea leaves into the pan. I wait for the water to deepen in colour before pouring in a dash of milk to make *doodhpatti*. I add my usual: a cinnamon stick, two pieces of cloves (good for sinuses), whole black pepper (good for digestion), and some fennel seeds. This is my amma's recipe from when she would make her own tea in the

Hashims' kitchen. The rest of the staff would drink the syrupy kind, with several spoons of sugar, but Amma would make me drink this with her. She said it was a recipe for good health. The fragrance takes me back there for a minute. I let the tea condense a little before pouring it in my mug.

Where are *you*, though? Didn't you promise you would come back for me? Didn't you promise, with tears in your eyes, when the police took me and Amma for questioning, that you wouldn't let anything happen to me? What happened? I imagine I was easily forgotten when life still offered you ease and an escape. Where are you now? Probably enjoying your sheltered life, perhaps even married to a woman more worthy of your status—one your family approves of too. I close my eyes and conjure up a face, curly hair, brown eyes, strong hands. I felt your warm arms around me when Bajjo was kidnapped. I felt your gaze upon me when you handed me that prized bag of *chorun*. I felt the tears running down your face as you held my hand tight that day. When I dug my fingernails into your wrist, my heart was beating so fast, I thought I would fall, too. Why did you never try to find me?

You were going to be in my life, and I was going to be in yours.

But, in the end, you were just like the rest of them, weren't you?

ZOHAIB

Cusco, Peru

The herb-shop guy spooked me out, no doubt, but I'm adamant not to read too much into things. Talha and I agreed it was probably a performance—he must say all sorts of vague but alluring nonsense to tourists all the time, and who isn't drawn in by that stuff when they're in a foreign land, where everything seems mystical just because it's alien? I laugh now, wondering how many gullible tourists have been duped into buying a magical potion because of his spell. It didn't quite work for me—I couldn't get out of there fast enough.

It's our second day of the trek and I already feel blisters forming on the soles of my feet. I'm wearing my newly purchased Timberland boots that I haven't had time to break in. They feel stiff on my feet and the ankle support is doing nothing. We come across a board on the mountain that says, *MOVING UP*. I feel a lump growing in my throat. Today, we are meant to trek for nine hours straight—eight for frequent trekkers, apparently—out of which six are on an incline. This is not some smooth slope incline, mind you—it's the real deal.

Talha is up ahead, leading the pack with ease next to the local guide, Alejandaro, who has taken to being called Alex. The group consists of four others: a German guy, Georg; Tatiana, from Sweden; Melanie, from Australia; and Chavez, from Guatemala. It's a good bunch, really. I lag behind with Tatiana. She's warm and open, and I felt an instant affinity towards her. To be honest, I'm surprised how comfortably I am speaking to her. She seemed to naturally gravitate towards me, too. She told me she's an intuitive healer. I'm not sure what that means, but she did say that she is able to "read people". Well, it wouldn't take any amount of skill to read how much I'm dreading this trek.

"Hey. C-Can we stop for a breather?" I call out to Alex, a little loudly, so he can hear me.

He doesn't.

"Hey! I need t-to stop for a breather," I try again.

We are in the middle of climbing a very narrow staircase up the side of the mountain, consisting of what looks like a million steps, and there is no way six people can make a stop here, as it would block other trekkers. At this point, Tatiana takes pity on me and reaches out to Alex, telling him to carry on and that she and I will follow in a bit. I mouth "Thanks" to her, breathing hard. Talha comes over, saying he will wait with me, but I wave him away and Tatiana insists she is happy to stay back with me.

My heart is pounding, and I can feel sweat trickling down my back. Right now, the weather is clement, but we were told it can go from warm to freezing within the day. Alex told us to pack our waterproof trousers and anoraks because rain was forecasted for today. I stand, leaning against the mountain till my heart rate gets back to normal.

"So, what's your deal? Wife? Kids?" Tatiana asks me, pronouncing kids as *keeds*.

"Ha! No, no wife, no kids. A sister, though," I say.

"That's nice. Parents?" she continues, curious.

My face darkens. This is not the easy small talk she thinks she is engaging in.

"I-In Pakistan," I say, curtly, clenching my palms into fists. I pick my walking sticks off the ground and prepare to climb again.

"What about the sister? Where does she stay?" Tatiana probes.

"She lives with me, in London," I say tersely. I feel my muscles tightening.

"What does she do, your sister?"

"I think we better get moving, you know, catch up with the group, don't you think?" I curl my lip—an attempt to smile—trying to keep it light, but it turns into a sneer.

"You're in pain, aren't you?" she asks, as I begin walking.

"Yeah, my knees are hurting a bit." I'm trying to wing it, but I know what she's asking. I'm not going to engage.

"No, I mean in your...What do you say? Heart? I can see you're struggling with something?" she says, like it's both a question and a statement.

What is it with people here? First that old man, now Tatiana. Yes, I'm hurting. I'm hurting so much that I sometimes want to stop feeling anything at all—I just go entirely numb. I'm hurting so much that there are days when a lump forms in my throat and constricts every word I want to say, like a powerful lock. Sometimes the pain is so intense, it feels like my skin will crack open from the pressure of everything I'm containing. Sometimes I forget where I am, and I panic. I panic that I have left Misha on her own and she may get hurt, and I can't let that happen again. I panic that I will stop breathing, and no one will be able to find me because, some days, I am completely alone. They will have to track my phone, and my phone will be off, and my parents—too busy dealing with their own grief, still, all these years later—will not know that I've stopped breathing.

"You know, it's okay to feel pain. Life will give pain, but life will give blessings too. It's the path you choose to take," Tatiana says, from behind me.

I want to close my ears, like children do, but I'm climbing a mountain, with walking sticks in my hands. I don't want to hear this. I don't want to face anything. My mind is struggling to keep the thoughts cohesive. They're jumbling up, now. I can feel it. My legs hurt, and there's this place, under my lungs, that's aching. I feel claustrophobic, even though I'm out in the open. Dark clouds are now gathering in the sky and their shadows will envelop me soon. It's getting windy and cold. I'm moving without thinking, my mind and body dislocating. I wish there were a pause button on my memories so I could collect my scattered pieces. My hands are gripping the hiking sticks and my ankles are hurting from the boots. I look up to inhale, but my lungs feel burdened. Several drops of cold rain hit my face. I should really put some layers on. I'm cold and wet, but I keep climbing up, up, up.

MISHA

"Ouch!" I squawk, for no apparent reason.

I'm not really hurt, but my elbows feel grazed. Mama puts some of the cream on my elbows from the white and orange tube that she uses when the weather starts getting hot. My dryness has a special name that I don't remember. I don't like the smell of the cream, so I usually hold my breath when the stink hits my nose. "Is it hurting?" Mama asks.

"Not really, but it's smelly," I say, making a face.

"Drama," Bhai says, styling his hair in front of the mirror. He has become taller in the past few months and has started being more irritating. He walks around like he's so much better than me. He straightens his shoulders a bit too much and sometimes it feels like the uniform he's wearing is on a hanger and not a body.

"Mama! Tell Bhai off! He never minds his own business," I complain.

Mama gives Bhai a stern look, but doesn't say anything.

"What did I do?" he asks, turning towards us. He goes back to fixing his hair when neither of us responds. He picks up his school bag—a plain navy Nike backpack, not like the graphic ones I prefer—and starts walking out of the door.

"Hurry, Mama! Bhai will leave me behind. He had Rasheed *chacha* drive around the block the other day, just so I would cry at the gate, thinking they had left," I say, scornfully.

Masi hands me a warm glass of milk and waits for me to finish it. There is a film on the surface of the milk, and I wretch a little, involuntarily. I drink half of it and hand it back. She also helps me put my school bag on my back.

"Finish your milk quickly and leave," Mama calls out.

I rush down the stairs before she can see the unfinished glass of milk. I find Nono waiting at the main gate.

"You haven't left yet?" I ask. She usually leaves half an hour before me and Bhai.

"No, van driver seems to be late today. Mrs. Farid will be so mad at me," she says.

I consider asking if we could drop her off, but I know, after we drop Bhai, it's my school time, and Nono's school is a bit far, so this might not work. I try to figure out a way in my mind to help her reach her school on time, but I can't see a way. I decide to drop it, otherwise we'll all be late.

"He will be here soon," I say confidently, like I know the van driver's schedule.

I scratch my elbows. There's a mixture of cream and blood under my nails.

Nono shrugs her shoulders and pretends to be looking for something in her bag. I can see brown patches of dirt on her white shoes. Her lanky body seems to be lost in her huge uniform, her sleeves way past her wrists. I look down at my smart starched white shirt and blue zip skirt. I wish Nono could have hers tailored to her size as well. I know Mama buys her a bigger size

102

so "it fits for two years," she once told Masi. I wonder if I have enough *Eidi* left over to buy Nono a uniform her size. The car is waiting outside the main gate and Bhai is leaning over to the driver's side, honking impatiently. I take one last look at Nono and walk towards the car.

MISHA

Karachi, Pakistan

Masi has a square face. Ever since she came to work for us, she has had wrinkles around her eyes and mouth. She has a big golden flower nose pin on her left nostril. She has been so sad for the past few months—always frowning, her mouth fixed upside down, like a cartoon. The wrinkles have always been there, from before Abida was kidnapped, and when her husband was still alive, but she would always smile wide whenever I spoke to her. Her hair was mostly black, in those days, with a few white strands and even some orange ones, from the henna she liked to put in. Nono didn't like the smell of the henna, but I liked it. It reminded me of fun times like Eid and weddings. Today, she is scrubbing the floors, her hair tied up in a bun with a dupatta around her head, like a warrior going to battle with the dirt. Her mouth is still a downward frown, her eyes dipping into their deep, dark sockets, looking like big holes on her face.

"Amma! Iqbal is here!" Nono yells from the veranda. "Rasheed *chacha* is saying Iqbal is here!"

Masi turns her head, clutching her chest. She seems to be ready for more bad news. I quickly begin searching the drawers of a cabinet, trying to look busy. A hair tie, extra batteries that probably don't work, a screwdriver. Who even uses a screwdriver in this house?

Both Nono and Masi have gone downstairs to see Iqbal, hurrying to hear what news he brings. Good or bad, I don't know yet. I think the coast is clear and I can leave the cabinet now. I begin tiptoeing towards the staircase. I want to hear too, but I don't want to be around if it's bad news.

Iqbal is invited in. Mama is not home. I don't know what to make of it. He has grown taller since he was here a few months ago, almost looking like a little man, with a stubble on his chin. Masi is crying; he is smiling. Nono is still outside.

Iqbal looks up at me and smiles. I can see all his yellow teeth.

"Thank goodness! Thank God! Thank the seven skies!" Masi is crying.

I peek from behind the banister. I don't see Abida. But I think this must be good news if Masi is thanking God with all her heart. I'm waiting for Nono, so she can explain everything to me, while Iqbal *bhai* keeps smiling at me. I duck a little so he can't see me anymore.

Nono's brother Iqbal used to come around often. He would do odd jobs around the house: clean this, fix that. He knew how to do a bit of electrical work, maybe plumbing too. He would also play with us—Nono and me. One time, we were playing catch-me-if-you-can, and Iqbal was on. He said, whoever he caught first, he would swing them, so we were both a little lazy in our running away because we also wanted to be swung around. He caught me, that time. So, he picked me up in his arms from my arm pits and began swinging me from side to side, jokingly trying to make me fall, lowering my body almost to his belly button'

'Now you can wrap your legs around me for a big one,' he said.

"What's that hard thing?" I asked him when I did as I was told.

"Oh, it's just my wallet," he told me, with a toothy smile. Most people have pockets on the sides of their trousers. His must have been different.

He continued to swing me from side to side.

"Bhai, I think you should go now," Nono said to him, quietly.

He stopped coming around the house, after that. Joined some "party," everybody said.

Nono is quickly climbing up the stairs. It must be good news. Her eyes are wet, but her face is happy.

"They found her! They found her in Balochistan!" she says to me, her face illuminated.

I don't feel so great, seeing Iqbal *bhai*, so I pull Nono's elbow so she can come on to the landing and tell me everything she knows.

"They found her at a *dhaba*. She called our relatives in Okara. My *chacha* went to pick her up. She's back home!" she shrieks.

"Is she okay?" I ask.

Nono's eyes cloud a little and she stops smiling. She bites her lip, like she hasn't thought about what three months of being kidnapped could do to a girl.

"I mean, I hope they didn't hit her or anything," I say, trying to sound hopeful.

I know kidnappers are bad guys who want money for the person they've kidnapped. They also sometimes beat people up, if they aren't given the money they asked for. I saw it on a TV show Mama was watching once.

"But I'm so happy she's back!" I say with enthusiasm, noticing that I might have made Nono sad. "Maybe she can come live with us!"

Masi walks in and gives Nono a hug before she can respond.

"She's back! Oh, she's back! A million thanks to God! A million!" she says, looking up at the ceiling.

Later that night, Masi takes out her packet of henna and tells Nono to put it on her hair. I smell it from far away when I go to the kitchen to grab a glass of water. I look forward to her orange hair in the morning.

NADIA

Lahore, Pakistan

"Daydreaming again, huh? You girls and your fantasies!" Faisal says, as he passes my desk.

He's kind of handsome, in a scrawny, unfashionable way. I quickly adjust my dupatta, letting a strand of my hair escape so it falls on my eyes. I am wearing a green *shalwar kameez*, with intricate lace detailing. Green really suits me—everybody says so. It has been a few days since Mubashir moved out of my house, and I feel light and free. I am not tied to anyone anymore. I don't have to pay for anyone else either. I try to think about him—probably passed out somewhere in his friend's house—and I feel no sympathy. I feel no remorse. I will be calling up Uzma's cousin, who is a lawyer, and asking how one makes it final in legal terms. I want to be legally single and unattached.

"Well, girls who have fantasies go places." I smile dreamily. Urgh, I didn't mean for it to come out that way. Shouldn't I be sad? I'll become a divorcee soon—isn't that something that is shunned in our society? Women who actively choose this path—aren't they villainized for life? What is this relief I'm feeling, then?

"Where were you for the past week, madam? I bet no one will even cut your salary!" Faisal says nonchalantly, now leaning over my desk. He has thick eyebrows and dark eyes. I think he is engaged again, but I'm not sure. I let my dupatta slip a little so that it rests on my shoulder. I don't make an effort to put it back on.

"Not your business. At least I don't have to work ten hours to get two hours' worth of work done," I retort, suddenly agitated.

Faisal raises his eyebrows appreciatively. He didn't really expect me to talk back. I feel a certain strength wash over me. I'm done being the *bechari*. The one to be blamed unnecessarily. To be shamed. Accused of not working hard enough, not being modern enough, being too modern. Blamed for just *existing*. I will not take it anymore. All the Mubashirs of my life will have to accept me for who I am. All the Faisals will know who they are messing with. I trace my finger on the corner of my desk, turning away from my colleague. He takes the hint and walks away.

I pick up the receiver of my intercom and ask to speak to Khursheed *sahab*. Better to tell him what happened with Shadab *sahab* before he tells him anything.

"Hello, *jee*, Khursheed *sahab*. This is Nadia...I'm sorry for calling you on your direct number...Yes. May I come into your office sometime today?...*Jee*. There was something I wanted to talk to you about...Thank you...Yes, *Khudahafiz*," I say, putting the receiver down.

There is a turning point in everyone's life, if they care to notice. My best friend left me, and I lost myself. Unloved things fade away. I don't want to end up like Abida *bajjo* did. Or Iqbal. I'm not ready to disappear yet. With every baby girl's birth, there is a measure of violence the world allots her. I reject this allocation of violence. Those who get comfortable with oppression do not change their lives. It is time I changed mine.

MISHA

"You know, Nono, you and I will get married together."

"That's silly—we can't get married to each other," Nono says.

"I don't mean *to* each other, I mean we will have a wedding on the same day."

"Hmm, but who will our husbands be, and what if they don't like each other?" Nono asks me.

It's a good question, but I don't think I'll marry a person who doesn't like Nono, because I would've known her for longer than him. If he doesn't like her, I will choose someone else to marry.

"And who will I marry?" She smiles sheepishly, as if she already knows who it is and maybe it's someone I don't like.

That thought disgusts me, and I make a puking sound.

"Hey, what did you do that for?"

"I'm just thinking that I won't marry someone you don't like, so you shouldn't marry someone I don't like, because that's only fair," I say, pouting, upset that I even need to say this to her.

"Well, I don't know who I will marry—Amma will decide—and I don't even know if I will marry in Punjab or here. Who knows? Maybe in a castle on top of a gorgeous mountain."

I don't like it when Nono acts like she knows everything—like she knows and thinks of things I don't. She likes to remind me sometimes that she remembers me being in nappies, to say she is older. But, then again, what she has said has worried me now, because what if we don't get married together, and she marries in Punjab, and I marry here, and we don't know each other in the future? That would be so sad.

"Nono, don't do that. At least try to agree. You can wear red, and I can wear white. We can both have tiaras, and we will wear silver heels—same design, so everyone knows we're sisters."

"I don't want to wear red. You wear red, and I'll wear white. And we are not sisters," Nono says, as a shadow crosses her face.

"Well, you know what I mean," I say, feeling bad because I know she is not my real sister, but I would have liked her to be.

Nono traces the white lace on her sleeve. She's wearing a *shalwar kameez* Mama gave her, years ago, for Eid. It's too fancy, with its lace trimmings and gold buttons, for an after-school chat in my room. I'm still in my uniform, but she has already changed and showered, even though she arrives home after me, in her school van.

"You know, here's a thought," she says, smirking. "I'm not your sister, but I could be your sister-*in-law*."

"What does that mean?"

"It means, if I marry Bhai—I mean Zohaib—it will be someone you like, and I won't even have to go back to Punjab. I can just marry here and live here with you."

I'm not sure how I feel about this suggestion. I kind of like the idea of Nono living here forever, but I'm also not so sure marrying

Bhai is right for her. It makes my tummy kind of squirmy thinking about Bhai and Nono together, when they already seem to be too chummy and leave me out. I think some more. Perhaps it won't be so bad once I have my own husband to play with, and Nono will still be a part of my life.

"Okay, but on one condition," I say.

"What is that?" Nono asks me.

"That only I wear white."

Nono smiles at me, and I'm not sure if she agrees or not, but I'm already imagining all the sparkling jewellery I'll be wearing, and the henna designs I'll be getting done. It'll be perfect. Now, I just need to find myself the right husband, who likes rabbits as much as I do…

ZOHAIB

Cusco, Peru

We finally arrive at the campsite, and I'm drenched. I didn't put my rainproof trousers and jacket on in time, and I ended up soaked through and freezing cold. I won't be going camping again in a rush. Talha feels bad that he left me behind, but I've assured him it's fine. I'm supposed to meet everyone for dinner at seven p.m., but I'm hoping to get some hot coffee before then. My body feels like lead, and I have no place to dry my clothes as the rain remains incessant.

I think about Tatiana and the questions she asked on the trek. It unsettled me. No one has ever probed like that or pushed me beyond what I have wanted to say. I know I've been hurting for a long time. Dr. Whitaker and I have been working hard for years, and I'd like to think we have made progress. But Tatiana probed in ways that pierced a hole in my memories and forced open old memories afresh.

Dad is sitting on the kitchen table where we have dinner together. Mama has locked herself in the room. She doesn't want to see me. She doesn't want to meet anyone. Dad hangs his head low.

113

I'm shivering. I must be cold, or am I crying?

I lie on my back on the camp bed, listening to the pitter-patter of raindrops against the tent. A worm crawls up my mattress—I flick it off. My teeth are chattering.

Why didn't you think about me, Mama? I was just a child. Did you really think I didn't need you? And Baba, you? You honestly thought sending me away was going to fix everything? Why did you think your grief was greater than mine? More complicated? And my sweet Nono, I'm sorry. I'm sorry for how Mama treated you. She was grieving. She was in a bad state. Sweet Nono, she feels sorry too, I'm sure. Just like I do.

"Hello? Hey, Zo? Are you in there?" a female voice calls.

"Yes," I muster.

"Zo? Are you okay?" Tatiana asks again, this time a bit louder.

"No. No, not okay," I whisper. I feel choked. I don't think she can hear me. I'm shivering and crying. I don't know if it's the cold or if it's the memory replaying through my limbs.

I hear Tatiana unzipping the tent. It takes a couple of minutes. The rain continues unabated. She's in, and she catches sight of me.

"Zo, it's okay. It's okay." She rushes over to me.

I'm crying uncontrollably now.

"Come here. Now, now." Tatiana tries to console me. She puts her arms around me, her face resting on my shoulder.

My ears are ringing, and my slow, silent tears have turned into heaving sobs.

"Zo, whatever it is, you'll get through it. I'm sorry if I pushed you. It's okay," she says.

Talha must have overheard or seen my tent open and made his way over. As he pulls back the entrance flap, I glimpse the clouds hanging low and a single lightning bolt slicing the sky.

"Zo, what happened? What's happening here?" He looks over at Tatiana accusingly, and then at me.

"No, no, it will never be over! Sometimes I see no end at all. I can only see death as my release. How else does someone get away from their past? I've tried running away, but the past just follows me," I cry.

"Do you want to talk about it? Is it your parents?" Tatiana asks.

My sobs are making me breathless. "It's Misha. It's her. I...I..."

"What did Misha do, Zo? What happened?" Tatiana probes.

"Maybe you should stop," Talha intervenes, and suggests Tatiana leave. "Zo, it's okay. You don't—"

"No. M-Misha, my sister. I made a mistake. I'm so sorry, Misha. I'm so very sorry."

The rain beating against the tent seems to have intensified. The wind is howling with it too. My heart thuds heavy in my chest and adds to the cacophony. Sweat gathers on my forehead, goosebumps on my arms. Needles seem to be pricking my fingertips. I scream.

Tatiana pulls away, afraid. She leaves under the glare of Talha.

I scream again from every inch of my body.

This time, Talha takes hold of my shoulders and cradles me, rocking me from side to side. "You're okay. I'm here, bro. I'm... *Shh,*" he says, tightening his grip.

I can smell grief in the air. I growl, and I want to tear apart my skin. "How could I do this to you, Misha? How could...?" I am beside myself. "How did I let you go?" I scream in between my sobs.

"You didn't, Zo—you didn't do anything. It wasn't your fault, everyone knows that. She had to go; it was her time, Zo," Talha says desperately, crying now too. "She's gone, Zo. You have to let her go for real, this time." Talha sobs with me.

"I killed her! I killed my sister, and I don't deserve to live. I killed my baby sister. What did I do? Oh, what did I do?" I put my face in my hands and keep crying and shaking. I can feel Talha's embrace hold me together. I cry until everything begins fading away. And then...Silence.

PART 2

GULSHAN

I fold the creases of the *shalwar kameez* I have just stitched. Sleeves outwards, collar central, double the fold. I neatly put the *jora* on the pile I'm almost done with. Just need to stitch the buttons. The lapels are unlike that of a coat—on a *kameez*, they are straight. I look towards the pile that is undone and heave a sigh. It's six thirty p.m. and I'm supposed to deliver these clothes by eight p.m. It's wedding season and everybody wants to wear velvet because it's trendy and expensive. Karachi winters are so mild, they don't do justice to the money spent on warm festive clothing, but these rich *begums* don't really seem to care. I usually just make clothes for the maids and servants, but this time I'm stitching a kaftan for Ghazala *baji*'s daughter. She is from a well-off family, but not as rich as appearances would suggest, so she has chosen to get her daughter's wedding clothes stitched by me. I can make the latest designs as good as the designers' first copy. I just haven't had my break yet.

The air smells of winter. It's only November, but work has already picked up. My Concern is the electricity bill. Somehow, the electricity company charges so much on my sewing machine, last month the bill was so high that it could only be usage of the machine increasing I want to hire an assistant now, and I have a fair idea about who that person could be. She just needs to get out of her head a little bit and embrace what Allah has planned for her. In her condition, she really should not be looking for work elsewhere.

The whirring of my sewing machine eases my nerves. I still have an hour, and only three more garments to go. My phone interrupts the hum of the appliance. I look up and pause; I don't want the cloth to be torn by the sewing-machine needle while I'm distracted elsewhere. It's a call from an unknown number, which could mean a new client. As busy as I am, I would never refuse a new client. New clients are Allah's blessings. That's how I keep the business growing. Next, I will put up samples of my work at Adeeb *bhai*'s tailor shop. If nothing else, maybe he will outsource some work to me.

"Hello, *jee*? Who is speaking?" I ask, putting the caller on speakerphone. I can't afford to take any breaks.

"Hello—is this Gulshan, the tailor?" she enquires.

"Yes, yes, *baji*, I'm Gulshan," I say enthusiastically. New client indeed!

"Good. Ghazala *baji* gave me your number. I need to get some work done. You were the one who stitched Shezi's *lehnga*?"

"Yes, I made it. I can stitch anything, really. What are you looking for?" You need to show enthusiasm, otherwise *bajis* will go to someone else.

"Well, lots of things. I need clothes for my maids. A shawl that needs a border stitched. Why don't you come to my house, and I can show you everything that needs to be done?" she says quickly.

"Okay, but it's late today. You can WhatsApp me your location. I will come tomorrow," I say, looking at the unfinished *kameez* I'm sewing. I need to wrap up, now.

"Okay, let me do that. But, please, can you just come today? Consider it an emergency," she says, almost out of breath.

It's *always* an emergency. An emergency requiring the stitching of clothes. People from my family would laugh. If someone was having a baby, back in our village, in Okara, we still wouldn't call it an emergency. Even in active labour, a woman would finish her day in the fields, picking cotton or rice, and then go home to deliver her baby. Sometimes, she wouldn't even call a *dai*—she would just take care of it herself. I chuckled slightly to myself.

"What do you say?" asked an obviously desperate *baji*.

"Just use this number. I have WhatsApp on it. I'll try, but no promises for today," I reply.

"Okay, I'll do that now," she says.

I hang up, but only then do I realize I haven't asked her name.

I save her number on my phone as *NEW BAJI*, and with that I get back to the important task of finishing my sewing.

ZOHAIB

I find myself staring at the e-invite on my phone for what seems like the hundredth time. The image makes me sweat and laugh in equal measures. It's almost ridiculous how fast things have progressed.

Faiza Usmani
Invites you
To the
Engagement Ceremony
of
Zohaib Hashim
&
Sumbul Qadir

As if on cue, my phone buzzes. The picture flashing on my screen is that of a pretty girl, just the kind you find on a roadside billboard or an advertisement: tall, thin, fair. The flawless Pakistani bride-to-be. I shake my head. A text appears; I slide the screen so I can read what it says.

Sumbul: *Excited???*

The message comes with several smiley faces, as well as red heart emojis. Sumbul is nineteen. Shahida Aunty convinced Mama that she is the perfect girl for me. Six years younger, and astoundingly beautiful, Sumbul doesn't have a single idea about who I am.

It has been two months since Talha and I cut our trip to Peru short and returned to London. It was an out-of-body experience. I say that because I literally had to come outside of my body to accept some things that had been happening to me. I had, for such a long time, refused to let Misha go, to accept that she was gone. I had kept her alive for myself, in my thoughts and imagination, so I could hate myself a little less. She still comes and talks to me sometimes, but I own my truth now. I am imagining her; she is not real.

After I got back to London, I felt physically and emotionally depleted. I was eager to speak to Whitaker again. Talha had booked me an appointment before we even left Peru.

As I entered his office, he welcomed me with more gentleness than he had in all the years I had been coming to him. Of course, he knew all along that Misha had passed away a lifetime ago, and I suppose the years of conversations with him meant that, when I was finally ready to accept this, it wasn't the total shitshow it would otherwise have been. I was glad to be in his office. There was a clarity to my vision now, even though I felt hollowed out.

"Zohaib, are you okay?" He left his chair to escort me to the sofa.

"Yes, doc. It's been a roller-coaster ride and I know that there are truths I need to face up to. I think I'm finally ready to do so," I said, before telling him everything that had happened.

Now, several weeks later, I sit, staring at the computer screen, confirming a one-way ticket to Karachi, Pakistan. Mama came to

London a few days ago, after Talha called her. Although they've never had a relationship, they have one thing in common: their love for me.

I'm still sore; my heart feels tender. I knew Misha was gone, and yet she was so alive for me. She filled my heart and home when I had no one. She helped me somehow stay alive.

Over the next few days, Mama helps me pack my stuff. I'm going to miss Talha, and even Dr. Whitaker. I promised I would video-call Whitaker. I hope we can stay in touch. Talha comes with us to the airport and Mama lets him take our luggage out of the taxi's boot and heave it onto a trolley. His nose ring shines under the deceptive London sun. I'm going to miss this guy. I want to tell him that, but the words get stuck somewhere in my throat.

We make our way through Terminal 3 at Heathrow. Checking in is nice and easy, and, with time to spare, we have a coffee at PretAManger. When we have two hours left to go before our flight, Mama decides it's about time we head through to the departure lounge.

"See you on the other side, bro." Talha tries to keep it light, but his voice breaks. There is so much we have lived through, so much love and pain between us, but he knows I need to leave this part of my life. We hug, I thank him for everything, and he promises to be there for the wedding.

Sumbul has been messaging me consistently and Mama insists I don't say too much. She knows I have my doubts, but is eager to get me to Karachi and into Sumbul's company. She is sure that is all I need to be convinced that marriage is the panacea my mother insists it is. I remain sceptical, but at this point I'm too worn out to make any decisions. Accepting Misha's death has been like tearing apart my most favourite limb—I don't even know if that makes sense, because all limbs should be of equal importance. My mind is speaking gibberish and I let Mama take my hand as I drag my one suitcase containing my life in London.

Once we are on the plane, Mama turns towards me. "Zohaib, I just have one request," she says, her eyes not meeting mine.

"What's that?" I ask, sipping the water from the plastic cup given by the air hostess.

"Don't call your baba right away. I don't want to keep you to myself, but I just...I just need some time processing all of this as well. I knew...well, I knew you were unwell; I mean..." She's trying to find the right words.

I feel you, Mama; there aren't any right words.

"I know you needed me. I just need a little time," she finishes, recovering herself. "People have been saying things to him. Things about you. I know this is all very sudden, but...but I had to do this. Sumbul will be good for us."

"I miss him, you know," I say, perplexed.

"I know you do. We'll figure out a way forward," she says, almost business-like now.

I look at her. My once beautiful Mama has aged beyond her years. In the absence of love, sorrow has carved its pattern on her features. Distance has perpetually marked its territory, so much that I think I've forgotten how to touch her. But she is here now. I cup her face in my hands, like a prayer, and say, "Mama, let's go home."

NADIA

Karachi, Pakistan

I roll on to my side, pulling the blanket over my head. A shiver runs down my spine as I trace the growing roundness of my belly.

"You're expecting," the doctor had said, looking at my blood work.

"B-But that's not possible!" I responded, trying to deny her statement away. I traced the thread border of my dupatta, a habit I'd picked up in my early years. The clinic was stuffy, with a small window and a rusty ceiling-fan for ventilation.

"Well, your blood report shows increased hCG levels. We can confirm with an ultrasound, but it certainly looks like it." She peered over her reading glasses. She had a square face, a bump along her nose making it look longer than it was. "When was your last period?" she asked.

"It was just..." I mentally calculated how long it had been. After separating from Mubashir, I had moved into a hostel in Faisal Town. The rent was easily manageable with my salary, since it had shared rooms, with three beds in each, and, after the whole incident with Shadab *sahab*, I had asked for a raise. The realization washed over me like a tsunami: I hadn't had my period since moving. I had been too busy to notice. It had been upwards of three months.

"Has your period been irregular before? Have you been experiencing any nausea?" the doctor probed, her tone slightly irritated. I assumed she dealt with a lot of cases where women and girls were oblivious to their pregnancies. Maybe their pregnancies were even out of wedlock. I shuddered at the thought.

The doctor recommended some tests and gave me vitamins to take regularly. There were a million thoughts that were racing through my mind. Should I tell Mubashir? Should I get an abortion? How will I pay for the doctor visits and delivery? How will I keep working?

I *had* been throwing up. Thinking back, it seems pretty ridiculous that I didn't realize it before, but I had put it down to a stomach bug of some sort. The first person I called was Uzma, and I confided in her.

"You know that there is no maternity leave at our office, right?" she said, worried.

I knew that. And I had already exhausted my leverage with the sexual-harassment incident by asking for a pay rise. They were not going to let me have maternity leave too.

"Well, they don't have to know now. You're not going to tell, are you?" I asked her, my tone accusatory.

"Of course not!" she promised.

As the months went by, it was harder to conceal the pregnancy. Eventually, I was called in to hand in my resignation. I needed an alternative plan. I couldn't afford to not work and keep staying in rental accommodation.

I turn to lie on my back, now. All positions are uncomfortable for me at this point. The baby girl, as the ultrasound—my only one so far—showed last week, kicks me suddenly. Her kicks don't hurt me, but she seems so active.

The earlier days of my pregnancy were lonely. Even though my roommates at the time were supportive and well meaning, most of them had no experience with motherhood and had no idea how to take care of me. I wanted to call Abida, but she had asked for money in the middle of my own crisis, and I never returned her call. Best to leave her out of it, for now. For a while, I transported myself to Misha's house. What would my life be like if that day hadn't happened? Would I have kept staying in their house? Would Misha have been my port of call? Would Zohaib have supported me, no matter what? Would I have been the woman I am today? They say, your circumstances make you who you are—did mine break me or make me stronger?

I feel the breakage more than any strengthening, right now.

I come out of my reverie to phone my cousin, Goshi—Gulshan—who moved to Karachi a while ago. As a kid, she was like a sister to me, since my amma took her in when her *saggi* mother died. Goshi has also been married and divorced. She has a similar story to mine: married to a drug addict, though her husband had the additional charm of being a wife beater too. I have to tell her everything. I have to tell her that I am alone with nowhere to go. She has a snug place, but there is lots of space in her heart, *jee*.

"Are you crazy? Of course, Nado! That is the best news I have heard in years! So much *rehmat* will fill my house! What a blessing it would be!"

I keep sobbing into the phone.

"Silly girl, stop crying! You will always have a home with me. Why would you even ask? You could have just shown up at my house and I would have given you my bed, my everything!"

"Goshi…I'm so happy to have you. I'm just so relieved. I have nowhere to go, Goshi; I've been on a sinking ship for too long!"

"Don't cry, Nado; your crying days are over, *kasam se*! You will live with me, and we will raise our future daughter together!"

I cry late into the night with relief, slowly releasing myself from the tensions that have been holding my body stiff. My hand rests on my belly, now. There is so much love and such little language to carry it. I don't know her yet, but I love her so much already.

I call her Emaan. What is *emaan*, really? Is it the desire to believe in a higher power? Is it an obligation, a forceful submission? Or is it an exquisite inclination to surrender to He who knows better? Do I need *emaan* back in my life, my faith, to carry on? Is that why I'm calling her that?

One last kick, and Emaan seems to have run out of energy. I sigh. Maybe I'll get some sleep, now.

GULSHAN

Karachi, Pakistan

I used to be jealous of Nadia. Whenever she would come back to visit us in Faridpur Sohag, with Bua, as I called her mother, she would tell us all kinds of fancy stories. Misha this, Zohaib that. She would talk about her fancy school, where everything was in English. Her books were in English, she could even talk in English! She was off being this *angrez*, while I was left with an adoptive family, the dreadful leftovers. Chacha, who was Bua's husband, was notorious for not sparing anyone in his bouts of rage. He would beat Iqbal up senselessly, and, after Bua left with Nadia, I became his punchbag too. Bua had always said he would never raise his hand to me, considering how much he loved my mother, but I guess people can be wrong about a lot of things. I had never visited "Misha's palace," as Nadia would call it—her "*mahal*." She would describe it in detail: a fairyland, with glass doors, flowers of every kind in the garden, and—oh, my Allah—the food she told us about! Nothing less than the divine *mano salva*! Absolutely exquisite! It was like she was in the Taj Mahal or someplace like that! She told me about dishes that I couldn't even pronounce correctly. The other servants treated her like she was some *begum* too.

I was mildly obsessed with the idea of Karachi. I imagined it to be fancy, like in the films we sometimes watched on the rented VCR. I knew I wanted to get out of Okara, and I did at the first opportunity that came my way. I was always good at stitching; I would stitch for the entire *muhalla*: Saeeda *masi*, Rubina *baji* in her new house, Bakhtawar near the mosque. Saeeda *masi's* husband owned a tailor's shop in Karachi. He saw my work and immediately offered me a job. He said all the expensive work was given out in Karachi; if I wanted to become something, it would have to be in the celebrated city of Karachi. It was a lifeline, after my divorce. I initially moved in with him and his daughter, Khalida, who was attending an embroidery workshop near Abdullah Shah Ghazi's mausoleum. Later, when work picked up, I moved into my current home.

All the while, I knew what was going on in Nadia's life through Abida *bajjo* or Bua. I met her at her father's funeral, at her wedding with Mubashir, and when we were both in Okara for Rubina *baji's* third baby. Nadia had exceptional strength. But she was also somehow misplaced between two worlds: the glossy world of the rich, and the lustreless reality of the hustlers. She had seen too much, too quickly, and her fall back into our lives must not have been entirely pleasant—especially after the way the Hashims treated her. I wished, then, that I could help her, but I knew I would be out of my depth.

When she called me with the news that she's having a baby, I heard her voice quiver for the first time. Like she was unsure. Of course, I would keep her, I said. Of course, I would help her raise her child. What Bua did for me, even when she had to leave me behind, was more than what a girl like me could ask for. Of course, I'd be there for Nadia.

I look at her now, sprawled on the *charpoy*, a mystical creature almost. She had made something of herself. She was successful. She was working in an office before coming back to Karachi. She no longer wears the hijab; instead, her hair is shorter. She even wears make-up. Not that she needs to. She is beautiful. Her sharp brown eyes accentuate her face, her oval face glowing, made perfect by her wide generous lips. Her beauty is not conventional—not the kind you see in magazines. Not like those stick-thin girls. She is voluptuous. I always saw her draped in layers outside the house; it feels like I'm seeing her body for the first time, seeing her body for what it really is—womanly, goddess-like. Her pregnancy seems to emphasize her beauty, giving her a gorgeous glow, heavenly and feminine.

I don't know if this baby will ruin her life, the life she's built so carefully, despite the trials and turmoil sent to her by our *Rabb*. But I know life has more in store for her—she will make it. Whatever she decides on, she will succeed. And, if I can help her in any way, I will. Right now, my mission is to get her busy. I want to win her interest in my tailoring work until she delivers. I will teach her the ropes and have her be my apprentice. On that thought, I shake her a little.

"Nadia? Nadia? Wake up. The sun has been up for hours. Wake up—I need your help." I make my voice sound chirpy. "*Utho beta, aakhen kholo*," I say in a sing-song voice, recalling a beloved childhood Urdu rhyme.

I look around the modest quarter I rent in Neelum Colony, a respectable two-room enclosure. I have good neighbours: Shahida *chachi* on the floor above, and Mehvish in the quarter next to mine. Sunlight enters the room through the corner window, making Nadia's face glow. She twitches a little and smiles in her sleep. Her innocence catches me off guard. This girl is going to have a baby. I remember her as a toddler, walking along the dirt-packed road leading to our house; I remember the room I shared with Nado and Abida *bajjo*, and how they made space for me in their home and their lives. She was a determined girl, this one.

She opens one eye and takes a peek at me. She surfaces from her slumber and then beams me a smile. "Do I have to? Don't unemployed people get to sleep all day? That's what Mubashir would do," she says, and lets out a dry chuckle.

I turn away from her and put a saucepan on the stove. The water quickly starts to bubble, and I put two spoons of tea in it. I remember, she likes her tea strong.

"I'm taking you with me, today," I say to her, over my shoulder.

The fan creaks as it attempts its lazy battle with the heat. A few mosquitoes buzz by; I swat at one with the palm of my hands. They come through the window. I should really get the net inserted. If I close the window, the room gets stuffy; if I open it, mosquitoes decide to crash our two-person party.

"My friend, Uzma, called someone she knows here in Karachi. She says I can work at a call centre. It's a few hours a day, and the pay is good. My stomach won't need to interact with anyone," she says wryly.

"How will you even go, in this condition? I'm not letting you take the bus. And where is this place, anyway?" I ask curiously.

"I don't know yet. I will call them today and find out. Trust me, I can't sit like this for two months. I had half a mind to call up a lawyer—you know, the one who handled my divorce—to get me some compensation. Who gets fired for being pregnant, *bhai*? The baby is not even disturbing them yet!" As she rants, her face seems to swell, or maybe I hadn't noticed the pregnancy weight on her face until now.

"*Acha*, then stay in and you can make food tonight. I need to deliver stuff and even visit this new client. Let's see how that goes," I say, rolling my eyes.

I pour the tea in two cups. Mine is a little chipped and the print on it is fading slightly. I hand Nadia the unchipped one.

She sips her tea and mulls over some thought for a few minutes. I can almost feel her deciding to accompany me, so she doesn't have to cook. The woman has serious issues with the kitchen.

"You know what? I'll make *gajar ka bharta*. I don't want to step out without a *chaddar* and have people X-ray me with their eyes. Get me a nice *chaddar* and I'll go out with you," she says brightly.

I smile and sip, contently. The thing is, I know Nadia came to me because she needed a place, but I've needed my sister for a long time. I have been lonely for an eternity. Maybe Emaan will bring joy to my life, too—a little miracle I have been missing in my life. A little bundle of blessings. I can't wait for you, little girl. I can't wait to hold you.

NADIA

I chop some carrots into long thin strips. There is a tree right outside Goshi's quarter, which some kind soul must have planted. I stare at it every day. It's reminiscent of one that stood in the grounds of the Hashims. Now, the fallen leaves move like a whirlwind of confetti.

I have memories of that day. They're foggy, but they're definitely there. Faiza *baji* called the police and they reached the house in the blink of an eye. Or maybe it was longer, but everything seemed so quick.

Amma was howling by then, as if she had lost her own daughter, and I wanted to remind her that I was right there, her Nado, but she seemed lost in her own world.

The police officers were sniffing around, and Faiza *baji* was hysterically pointing towards me. I tried to stay calm, but it seemed clear that this waking nightmare was yet to deliver more blows. I was digging my nails into my palms when an officer came close to me and grabbed my hands. I don't know what kind of law lets you treat a child like that, but it seemed it was the law of the rich. As an adult, I have been so enraged by this. I have looked it up and found out, under section 54 of the Code of Criminal Procedure, you only need reasonable suspicion to make an arrest. Reasonable from whose perspective? I wonder now. It was certainly not reasonable from mine. Of course, I did not know that at the time, but, just as the police put handcuffs on my small wrists, my Amma, in a desperate, ill-thought-out attempt at rescuing me, did the single most reckless thing: she told the police she did it.

Both of us were taken away in a grilled van to Tipu Sultan Police Station. I wondered, from the back of the ragged vehicle, whether Amma would be in jail with me. I had only heard of Nawaz *chacha* being taken away once, for theft, but his children stayed with Chachi. At the time, juvenile courts in Karachi were also just a legal idea to be implemented in the future. No rehabilitation centres or trial courts existed at the time, but, thankfully, things never got to that.

I remember the unbearable stench of urine was the first thing I noticed when they locked us up. Then, the sounds: a police officer tapping his foot, *tap tap tap*; the fizzle of the light bulb flickering; Amma's repressed cries; the cries from other cells in the night.

There were two women sharing our cell. One was old, with white hair spilling out of her *dupatta*, and black teeth, snarling at Amma. The other one looked a little over eighteen, her nails long and eyes dark. The prison cell was small, a single tube light shivering on and off, blinking against bare, grey, cracked walls.

"Amma! What did you say to them? Tell me! Why did you lie?"

Amma's face was in her hands, she was shaking. Her clothes were dirty, even torn—something may have happened in the van when she was trying to get closer to me. What a mother does to stay close to her blood.

136

"Amma! What will they do to us? Amma, talk to me, please," I said, my voice small.

"*Beta*, I had to. I'm so sorry. You're here because of me. I should never have left Faridpur Sohag. I should never have brought you to Karachi," she said, beating her chest.

"No, Amma! No, it's not your fault."

"I couldn't let them take you from me, my *chaand*. I have already lost one daughter's innocence, I couldn't let that happen to you." Her eyes were spilling tears. "There is little difference between the criminal and the police. We just have to wait for *reham* from our *Rabb*. Shh...I'm here, see? Never going to leave you, my *gurya*, never," she said, pulling me close to her.

The three days I was there, we slept on the dirty floor without a sheet or a blanket. I had no idea how to behave or what to do. I stayed close to Amma and tried to pray to a God we both believed in. We recited *Ayat-ul-Kursi* till our tongues were swollen and our throats dry.

After my time there, I felt as though I had been dropped into a perpetual labyrinth I could not escape. Life became unrecognizable. What did I do? I replayed the last moments of Misha's life repeatedly; with each remembering, my heart felt further hollowed. How was I going to fill this emptiness in my heart once more? I never had anyone help me with my grief—the loss my friend, my home, my life as I knew it, my future as I had dreamed it, Zohaib. I wanted to shout, *What about me? Who will help me? Who will I be?*

You know when I say I remember the sounds? The only sound I don't remember hearing was the sound of me crying. Because I never did.

*

137

Karachi is full of disclaimers, like a warning label on a pack of cigarettes. Karachi hits you hard with its smells and sounds— the *drun-drun* of the rickshaw, the sing-song voice of the news-channel anchor, the honking of the impatient drivers, the *tap tap tap* of beggars on the windows of shiny cars. I wonder what Emaan will be like, growing up in this city. Its beguiling glitter and its unglamorous truth. Will she be strong and fierce? Will she settle for what's apportioned to her, what she's told to do?

I wonder if she will meet someone like Zohaib, meet someone so early in her life, she will think he is perfect in every way...until he isn't. Will she study in another country? Work at an office? Will she have friends to celebrate her birthday with? Will she ask me where I come from? Who her father is? For now, I've decided not to tell Mubashir anything. What can he offer my daughter, anyway?

Since I've come to Karachi, I have thought about Zohaib more often. Misha has always been a part of me, since the day I lost her and before, but Zohaib exists in the Karachi air. I imagine I've seen his face in every man of about his age who passes me. I wonder what I would say to him. What does he look like? What would he think of me, with my expanding belly? I torture myself wondering if he even remembers me now, or am I just someone he passed by in life—a mere supporting character among a cast of rich and beautiful people? Life is a conundrum of chance and destiny. In truth, I don't know what I'd do or say if I ever saw him. But what are the chances, in a city of fourteen million people, that we would ever meet again? Does life allow second chances like that? I'm not convinced it does. It was so cruel with my first chance.

It's confusing, this life. How does one fill the void of a lost loved one? Did I miss Abida *bajjo*, my real sister, more when she was taken away, or did I feel for Misha more? How have I managed to come this far, when in that moment I thought I would die too?

I'm grateful for Gulshan. I'm grateful for this life inside of me, this breathing, kicking life that I can't believe belongs to me and me only. And I'll give you a good life, my love—I won't let anyone treat you any less than you deserve.

She kicks me in agreement.

ZOHAIB

Karachi, Pakistan

I wake up before the sunrise, before the birds, before everyone. There is something special about Karachi mornings, especially at this temperamental time of year. Nana's house has always had this haunting quality to it. It was magnificent in its time, built by the city's best architects and designers. I have memories in this house from when we would visit Nana and Nano as children. I recall the mulberry tree belonging to the house next door, which hung over so low into our garden that we could just jump and pull juicy burgundy mulberries from it, distributing the loot among all the cousins. Rehan, Anaya, and little Danyal would get plastic bags from the kitchen and collect all the fruit to be devoured later. As the eldest, I was the ringleader, and they would follow my instructions diligently.

I don't bother with breakfast. I'm staying upstairs in one of the guest rooms. It's a well-proportioned space, with two windows for cross ventilation. The mulberry tree is visible from one of the windows, though sadly there is not much fruit on it at this time of year. My suitcase is still unpacked, as if I don't plan to stay here long. *Where else do you plan to go, Zohaib?* Home, this onslaught that is Karachi, brings up all kinds of sentiments.

I hastily change into my running gear: thick-heeled running shoes and lightweight shorts. Over the years, Talha would sporadically get me to go jogging. I was not a good sport about it, but now nostalgia gets me up and running most mornings, and I cannot deny how good it is for my physical and mental health. I can see Talha's smug face and hear his victorious voice saying, *I told you so.* I smile and, with my shoes still untied, I speed down the stairs into the foyer, where I quickly tie my shoelaces sitting on the settee placed next to the main door. Stretching my hamstrings, I peer into the darkness of the house—the only light is the one on the main gates, far away.

For a moment, I imagine a different life for myself. I was intelligent, confident, a leader. I would have made a good businessman, just like Baba. Or a mathematician, maybe even a banker. I had plans. Who knew life would take such a violent turn?

I blamed myself then. I blame myself now, too. I had recurring dreams about her. Nightmares, every night, accentuated by Baba's desperate attempts to speak to Mama in the aftermath of it all. That, too, through the locked door of her room. I remember Nono and Masi being taken away. I remember banging on Mama's door afterwards, banging and banging. Asking her to open the door, just for a minute. A second. Everything else becomes a blur afterwards.

The next memory I have is in Manchester. I'm staying with Farrukh Uncle, who I only know as Baba's childhood friend who we met on his occasional visits to Pakistan. He doesn't have children; his wife is a doctor. I spend my weekdays at the boarding school in London and come to Farrukh Uncle's place at

141

weekends. I'm not mad. I'm not crazy. But I have palpitations. I guess I had no way to deal with the loss and a part of me thought, if I could just have her back in my life, I could stop feeling so damn sad all the time. I may have mentioned Misha once or twice to my teachers at school. The school counsellor got involved and shared their concerns with Farrukh Uncle, who at that point was my legal guardian in the UK. When he relayed this information to my parents, Baba threw more money towards my "welfare" and that's how I was introduced to Whitaker. Hence, the story of my first real relationship, after Talha, in London, and my long, slow march towards processing what I had endured.

To be honest, I hated Mama for a long time. The way she treated me after Misha's death. The way she treated Nadia. We were children; we didn't know any better. It was like she became judge and jury herself and pronounced us both guilty, sentencing us both to exile. I was shipped off to the UK, and Nono...I don't know where to begin. There was no one for me to ask, no way for me to enquire. I know Mama was grieving, but surely, she could have directed this cruelty somewhere else.

For a long time after, she didn't speak to me. I was sent away, and the truth is, after a while, I didn't want to speak to her either. And Baba—oh, dear Baba. He lost everyone. He told us to always think. To observe. To give things a chance, another chance. To not judge by how things appeared. The tippler pigeons. They were not what they seemed. I wish he had said something. I wish he had given *me* a chance. He lost each one of us in his failed attempts to keep his family together.

I resented them both—Mama and Baba—and, even as their calls became more frequent over the years, it only increased my disdain for them. There were many times in life I wished things had happened differently. I wish even now that Mama had not sent

142

Nadia away. I wish Baba had let me stay back with him. I was a child; I needed my parents. My release from the unhealthy coping strategies I built for myself has given me pause to reconsider my parents and their reactions. Misha is no more, but my parents remain—I could at least try to rekindle that relationship.

My relationship with Mama is nowhere near what it used to be. I have no expectation that it will be. I only hope we can build one at all. She has slipped into the role of mother-who-knows-best quite naturally, though. She has grieved for as long as I have, in her own way, and the lure of parenting a child in flesh and blood—albeit now an adult—is proving healing for her. But Baba—how do I find a way back to him again? I need him to be my baba once more, to guide me, to teach me. I want to tell him too, *Baba, our Misha is no more, but I'm here now.*

Five days until the official engagement. It almost seems unreal that I'm in this predicament. My heart is not in it, but I feel incapable of resisting anything, right now. Meeting Sumbul did not have the lightning effect Mama had anticipated it would, but I also don't want to decide anything for myself for the time being. I've decided to let Mama run the show, though I know I want Baba involved. He can't miss his only child's engagement.

I stuff a couple of napkins in my pocket. The air can be a little chilly during my early morning runs and my nose gets runny. I think about Nadia, about searching for her on Facebook, Instagram, LinkedIn. It's childish to think that I'd find her on any social media. What even was her surname? But I make a mental note to try nonetheless once I return from my run. With that thought, I pull the brass handle to the main door of my nana's house and quickly walk out.

The wind rolls over me. I feel my feet go numb in the first kilometre, my body just getting used to the sensation of movement. I square my shoulders; my steps begin to pick up speed. I push my body forward, and my mind focuses. Running is a tough exercise—the only one I've managed to establish since my move to Karachi. There is no destination, no finish line. You run kilometre after kilometre and don't really know what you're running for, or why. The only thing you can feel is your own breath and that intense sense of doing something purely for yourself. The sky starts to colour with deep shades of purple and orange. The sun emerges slowly at first, and then, almost suddenly, brightens up the sky. It's bright, but not blinding yet. I see very clearly, on the electric wires, sitting idly, the tippler pigeons. I imagine they sit here every day for hours, or maybe what seems like hours to me.

Remember to observe. Things are not always what they seem, echoes Baba's voice in my head. I know what I have to do now. I must speak to him. He must know I'm back.

FAIZA USMANI

Karachi, Pakistan

It was a quiet day. A silent September morning, the clouds of Karachi pregnant with post-monsoon moisture. The air smelled sour, as if it were whispering its discontent with what the day's happenings would conclude. A while ago, I had a brief stint with piety. I affiliated myself with an Islamic organization. It was nothing political, as some imagine these things to be. It was primarily focused on charity. I covered myself in a *chaddar*, a tad less overbearing than the burqa. I prayed five times a day and hosted regular *dars* at my residence. But, as the children grew older, I found myself getting distanced from religion. I gradually became more, as they say, liberal. I no longer prayed *Fajr*, occasionally even missed my *Isha* prayers. Masood was immersed in work, yearning to take back all that he had lost when his father passed away in his late forties. I married him after he had been completely abandoned by his elders. With the passing away of his father, he lost not only his mentor, but the factories owned by him, which were ruthlessly usurped by Masood's uncles. My father guided him, helped him build his business from scratch and turned him into a force to be reckoned with in business circles. Of course, Masood was sharp and resourceful in his dealings and quickly readjusted his lens.

I had put on nail polish that day, no longer considering if my *wuzu* would be valid. I even got a blow-dry done; daring not to wear the scarf, I lay the *dupatta* on my head or on my shoulder depending on the occasion. I was in a hybrid state—part religious, part my own interpretation. Misha was too young to adapt to either. She had always been an easy child. Her spirit was almost infectious. She had a big heart; she wanted to love till the lines blurred for most people. She was infatuated with that little girl, Nadia. I look back in lament, now, at my decision to take her in. The timid little creature, clinging to her mother's leg, her almond-shaped eyes strikingly beautiful even at the tender age of six, or maybe seven? I had never taken in a maid's child before, but then I'd never really had to. Most of the maids I'd had before were either Filipinos or local women without kids. I used to hire maids on this one condition: that they have no dependants—at least not physically attached to them. I couldn't afford any unnecessary ruckus in my house. I was nervous about that hiring, but excited about the prospect of a project, a good deed. No matter that I didn't cover myself the way I used to, I could still make a difference in someone's life and gain God's pleasure. And maybe I'd be forgiven for turning away from my duties of hijab. Little did I know that this seemingly harmless creature would be the one who would cause the most precious part of my life to be taken away from me. For her to be chosen to stay alive and my darling Misha to be taken away.

For years, I had trouble facing the truth. I blamed her. I turned her and her mother into the police. Having them arrested was no problem, but when lack of evidence threatened to let them walk free, I had my dad help keep them imprisoned through his contact with the Sindh Police. But in the end I dropped the charges, so the poor girl was not taken away for life. Ultimately, I didn't want her life to be ruined. It wasn't as if it would bring Misha back.

It wasn't yet the Basant season, a festival that was celebrated over all of Pakistan, but our neighbourhood, a lavish one, with rooftops of grand houses stretching out far and wide, didn't wait for it to be March to celebrate kite flying. Zohaib would go up to the roof in the evenings—sometimes chaperoned, other times just by himself. Most days, Zohaib and the other neighbourhood boys would have a flying competition. The *manja*—the sharp thread used for kite flying—was banned years later, thankfully, but not before my Misha was gone. Although it had nothing to do with the incident, I forever hated kite flying after that fateful September. I also began hating the sight of spinach and grapes, Misha's favourite vegetable and fruit. I started detesting evenings and the smell of baby powder and the sound of a child giggling.

I was not home that evening. I can't believe my Lord let me leave the house. I can't believe I didn't get to say one last goodbye to my sweet child. The last conversation I had with Misha was about how she was not getting the grease out of her hair, because she had recently decided to start showering herself. I had shouted at her, told her she would get lice and we would have to shave all her hair off. It wasn't her I was upset at, really. Masood's sister had taunted me the day before about my clothing preferences and my "charitable escapades," as she had called them. How the two didn't match, how my personality was a mismatch…How does one describe the day one loses one's child?

In those days, Zohaib was insisting I increase his pocket money. He was planning to set up shop for his cousins.

He wanted to "invest." He wanted to buy something so he could display his products—a shelf, like in the newly opened supermarket, Jumbo, on Tipu Sultan Road. Zohaib had always been ambitious. He was sharp and business-minded, like his father. He loved Misha, but he was also jealous of her, as siblings often are. He forever complained that she never got into trouble. He found ways to bother her. Since he was older and smarter, he would get her into situations, and she would guilelessly agree to be put in them. Before Misha was born, I had yearned for a daughter, so my family would be complete. She arrived, smiling, not a care in the world. It was not that I just wanted a little companion for myself; there was something brilliant about her. Yes, every mother thinks that about their child, but Misha, she really was special.

I had picked up my purse and given instructions to Masi to set the trolley, so that, on my return, everything would be ready to entertain guests—Masood's cousins, who had hijacked the family business after his father passed away—arriving from Faisalabad. Maybe it was the anxiety of hosting them, or just misgivings of a generally bad week, but I had not kissed Misha goodbye. That day, I did not take her along with me like I usually did if I had a kitty party. I hung my purse on my shoulder, my temper fuming at her hair being greasy.

I came back to the worst, most hateful evening of my life. Zohaib was hysterical. He was sitting in a corner, slapping himself and weeping uncontrollably. Masood was already home. I remember everything, every insignificant detail, with accurate precision. I remember the chandelier being turned on, the one we only switched on when there was a dinner party. An ambulance siren had remained on, a constant wailing in the air. They had forgotten to turn it off and nobody asked them to. There were a lot of white sheets; Misha lay on one, another one covered her body up to her chin. Her face was calm as if taking a nap, but I knew my baby was already gone. I may have fainted multiple times that evening, insisting on taking her to the hospital. Refusing to believe that my baby, my precious, my little girl was gone. Just like that. Just like that.

Everyone in the house was crying. Shah Zaman, Masi, Masood, Zohaib. The only exception was Nadia. She was standing next to the veranda door. Just standing. Her eyes were cast downward, but they remained dry. No show of grief. I remember, after waking up from one of my fainting spells, I locked eyes with her. The guilt. I was sure I saw so much guilt.

When I took Nadia in, my intention was to do a *naiki*. I was going to improve the prospects of this poor girl. She would be educated and away from the claws of misfortune that scratched at her family. I was going to make a difference. Every plan and intention I had made came crashing down, that fateful evening.

If I regretted my decision to take Nadia in as a child, I regretted what I did to her the day of Misha's death even more. I blamed her insistently. I was adamant she had more to do with my Misha's passing than Zohaib was ready to tell. I couldn't forget her eyes. I couldn't shake off the guilt I had seen in them.

It has been seventeen years, two months and four days since my Misha was taken from me. My marriage collapsed; the one person I shared everything with, I pushed him away. I hated myself. I hated Nadia. I hated Zohaib. I didn't know what to do with him. I had failed. I had failed as a mother, and I had failed as a human. I have had to let go of my anger towards my son. He's back and I still haven't let him speak to his father yet. He's not the little boy I last saw, and not a trace of the child he was before Misha's death seems to exist. I ruined that for him. But he's still more put together than I am. And Masood—oh, Masood—I still have trouble looking at him. Misha had so much of him in her. One day, I will learn to forgive. And, one day, I may begin to forgive myself. Just not today.

GULSHAN

Karachi, Pakistan

Nadia gawks at everything. Maybe she's trying to remember Karachi from her childhood, but then she was never out and about with Bua. As far as I know, she has never even been to Quaid ka Mazar. I toyed with the idea of taking her to experience the real Karachi—Burns Road Haleem, Empress Market, Kotari Parade, Zahid Nihari, the list could go on—but, in her current condition, it is important to take it slow. Plus, I still have to meet the new client Ghazala *baji* referred to me. Carefully tucking my purse under my arm in an effort to conceal it from pickpockets, I lead Nadia to the A30 bus to get to Defence—one of the most developed posh residential areas in the city, full of two-storey houses. I would have taken a rickshaw, but I still haven't received payment for the clothes I delivered this week. I know I should probably not risk taking Nadia on the bus, but she insists she's okay. At least she's not going to be alone.

"Are you sure you can hop on the bus?" I ask, feeling guilty for bringing her along.

She assures me it's fine.

"By the way, I'm really glad that you're coming with me to meet the new client. Your English might even make a good impression on her," I smirk.

She just smiles and rolls her eyes.

We reach the bus stop. I wave my hand excitedly at the ornamented public bus approaching us. The exaggerated poetry and paintings spread all over the bus are an ordinary sight for me, but Nadia, who is now more used to the plain Lahori Metrobuses, smiles at it with fascination.

"We used to go to Saddar in these, you know. Amma would not leave the house often, but I remember this one time when she took me to Zainab market to get a pair of jeans. I wanted a pair just like Misha's. Um..." Her voice catches a little and she quickly looks away, as if to stop herself from saying something she might regret later.

The bus stops two feet away and the conductor gestures for us to climb aboard. I go in first, extend my hand to Nadia and pull her up.

I know Misha died. I know Nadia had a complicated relationship with her. But, after she returned to our village, she never mentioned her name again. Not once. It was almost like Misha never existed. Bua told me Nadia was there when Misha died. It must have been traumatic. I've lost a lot of people in my life, but none of them died in front of me. And I was never accused of causing anyone's death. I say that because I know the police took her and Bua in, on the insistence of Misha's mother.

After getting off this bus, we need to take another to reach the intersection. From there, it should be no more than a ten-minute walk to the client's place—maybe fifteen, considering Nadia's pace. I've got the number down on WhatsApp: 192/II, Khayaban-e-Muhafiz. No street number though.

"Are you okay?" I ask Nadia again, once we're on the second bus. Her face looks ashen; there are small beads of sweat collecting on her forehead, now.

"Yes, just a bit light-headed. A walk should help," she replies, taking a deep breath in. She takes off her *dupatta* to reveal beautiful strands of dark brown hair, neatly tied in a braid, fastened with a maroon elastic band. Some strands of hair are spilling out from the sides, framing her flushed oval-shaped face.

"Maybe I shouldn't have brought you along on the bus," I say again, now really regretting my decision.

We eventually get off the second bus. It's a beautiful walk from there to the client's house. There are little patches of lush green grass and colourful flowerbeds outside the houses. Some houses have red sliding rooftops. The roads are mostly clean, except for a couple of empty plots where people have decided to dump all their trash. It's yin and yang: the stunning mansions and the dirty, empty plots. We walk along the pathway, crossing the main roads a couple of times to get to Muhafiz. I think I've been to a house in Muhafiz before but can't seem to recall the baji's name. Nadia is reading the address plaques out loud: "That's 190/I, 190/II. This one—192. Oh, it's 192/I—so, the next one…Wait, 192/I, oh." Her tone changes suddenly. An uncertain look crosses her face, her eyes fixed on the gold and brown gate as we approach it.

"What happened?"

She suddenly doesn't look too well.

"Nothing, nothing. You go, I'll wait outside." She looks pale, and stands, holding her stomach. She must be feeling sick all of a sudden. Too sick to move.

What is happening to her?

"What? No way. I didn't bring my cool cousin to let her sit outside. No, you must come in with me. You don't have to do anything, but you need to stay where I can see you, especially in this state." I am stern with her.

I know there is something wrong with Nadia, but we're too far out to return now. She is drained of colour and hesitant to go in. I gather my strength, reach out, and ring the bell.

ZOHAIB

Karachi, Pakistan

I stare at my phone for the thirtieth time. I haven't been counting, of course, but I'm pretty sure I've looked at the phone more than I've looked at Sumbul. The café we are in has a quaint outdoor set-up. It's 12:30p.m.—brunch time—but the fairy lights around the planters are on. They have those glow bulbs that seem to be in vogue these days, hanging from a wooden installation above us, giving the place a festive vibe. Most tables are occupied with people in twos and threes, while there is one big table with close to ten women chattering excitedly—and, might I say, rather loudly.

"So then I said, 'Mama, come on, I'm not going to wear olive green on my engagement.' I mean, I know it was just the dupatta's border that was a bit outdated, but I totally refused. No way! Nada!" Sumbul is a die-hard *Narcos* fan. She once told me proudly that she had picked up some words from the show.

"Uh-huh of course." I am now visibly distracted.

"So…have you decided on your clothes? Like, are you going traditional or wearing a suit? I know we don't have enough time to get a nice Zara or Paul Smith, but I can hook you up with a local designer, maybe? Their cuts are to die for. Of course, Papa will have to pull some strings, as it's short notice, but it's totally worth it," she says, confident that vanity is the only thing that matters—or should matter.

"Um, what?" I look up. She's got such a pretty face: heart-shaped, perfectly sculpted brows, a dimple on the right cheek. She's painted her lips pale pink, and her cheeks match the hue. She has a small mole above her upper lip; it's almost too perfect.

"Oh, you dreamer! I have to repeat everything twice. I was talking about your clothes. Also, Faiza Aunty said it's going to be a small event, so I don't know how I'll cut down all the people I need to invite! I mean, they'll be so mad at me if they find out I got engaged and never invited them!" Her eyes light at the mention of the engagement.

I'm waiting for Baba to call back. I called him right after my run, but there was no answer. Baba has always been an early riser. Though, I don't know if he still is—perhaps his habits changed while I was away. On seeing that there is no missed call or message, I open up Facebook and think to type "Nadia" in the search bar.

"Earth to Zohaib!" Sumbul is visibly irritated now. "I said, would you mind if I invited five more from my side? I mean, I know you haven't been around Karachi in a while; maybe I can take your guest list too, pretty please?" She is sticking her lower lip out like a child.

Oh, God—she is a child. I don't mean to be rude to her. Doubts start creeping over me again. Don't get me wrong, Sumbul seems like a lovely girl. Any guy would be lucky to marry such a beauty, and from a family like hers. But can she handle marrying me and all the baggage I come with? Does she have any idea about what's happened to me? I don't know what her mother has told her about me, but has she forgotten to mention that I've really struggled in the past? That I may find it difficult to sort through my feelings again?

I know I promised Mama not to take my past into my future, but, as much as we may talk about "chapters" in our lives, human beings are not books. We can't draw a line under our life experiences and expect to move on as though it never happened. The ink of our lives is wilder than that of a book. The ink of our stories seeps through the paper, bleeds over the confines of a chapter, drips over the edges of a page. It's not fair on Sumbul that I sit with her here, now, while I search for Nadia on Facebook. I open my mouth to say something, but we are interrupted by one of the raucous ladies brunching at the table nearby.

"Hi! Oh my God! How're you doing, *beta*? My, my! What a gorgeous top you're wearing! And who might this be? Is this the fiancé everybody is talking about?" the lady asks, eyeing me. She seems to be in her late forties, her hair up in an elegant chignon, her ears gleaming with diamonds. She has a wide nose, with yet another gleaming flower stitched to her left nostril.

"*Salam*, um, hello. I-I'm Zohaib." I extend my hand and take it back quickly. It's Karachi, and it may not be appropriate to shake hands with an aunty.

"Haha! It's okay. I'm not one of those conservative ladies who can't touch *na-mehrams*!" She laughs and extends her hand towards me.

I'm nervous to be seen outside my comfort zone. I'm not used to socializing. Sumbul seems to attract people wherever we go. Although we have hung out only three or four times with each other, I still feel nervous around her.

The woman turns her attention back to Sumbul.

"You're glowing already, darling! That mother of yours is taking you for the right facials, I see!" she says admiringly.

"Oh, Aunty, stop. I haven't had a facial in, like, two months. I'm just sticking to a vegan diet till the engagement," she says, gesturing at her all-green salad.

"Well, whatever it is, you must give Naila some tips. Anyway, I better get back—don't want to disturb you two lovebirds!" she says, and turns around before either of us can bid her goodbye.

We stand for a few seconds and then clumsily resume our seats.

"Well, that was a bit awkward. I, um, dated her son last year," she says, looking at me as if I would show signs of disapproval. Admitting that you've been out with another boy is a risky decision in Pakistani society, but it seems like more of a slip than an actual admission.

My phone rings suddenly and I leap across the table to answer it.

"Baba?" I say, without even checking the caller ID. I excuse myself from Sumbul and walk towards the café door.

"No, *beta*. I thought I told you not to speak with him yet," Mama's voice reeks of disapproval.

"Yes, Mama, but I think it's time. I need to see him, and I don't want it to be at the engagement. I need to speak to him; he must have heard I'm in town and will be wondering why I haven't contacted him. I listened to you—I am listening to you in everything. You know I'm not ready for marriage, but I'm still agreeing with your plans, Mama. Just don't push me on this too, *please*."

"Can we talk about this at least, when you get home?"

"Yes. B-But don't pressure me on this one, Mama—it's Baba. Please."

158

"I need to talk to you about something else too." Mama hesitates for a moment. "I'm not a hundred percent certain…I don't know…" Mama's voice cuts off a bit.

"What is it?"

"It's best that you come home, so we can talk." With this, the line drops.

I walk back inside, passing the ladies' table, half of whom are whispering to one another and casting meaningful coy glances my way. I ignore them and carry on to my table.

"Um, Sumbul, would you mind if I get my coffee to go? Mama needs me at home. Sorry." My apologies are almost becoming a habit, now. I peek at my phone again. The home screen lights up with a picture of me with Baba, in Paris. I'm eight in the photograph.

"Sure!" Sumbul says brightly.

I call for the bill and open Facebook again. Results from a previous search are still there…

Nadia Jamshed

Zenia Nadia

Nadia Kamran

Nadia Qureshi

Was it *Anwar*? Her dad's name?

More are loading. I click on *Nadia Anwar*. A lady is sprawled on a sofa chair, her eyes blue, an unnatural colour—probably contact lenses. Nope, not her.

I should maybe try calling some numbers. Masi's? I know she passed away a while ago. I don't have any of her sisters' numbers either.

"Hey, you're okay to drop me off though, right?" Sumbul asks, her perfect eyebrows raised in a plea.

"Yes, of course," I say. I don't know how much longer I can carry on with this pretence.

Sumbul gives me a tight-lipped smile, and we both walk towards my car.

SUMBUL

When I was young, all I wanted was to get married. I would watch videos for hours on end and plan my wedding down to the last detail. The last video I watched was only a week ago, just before the engagement.

Sometimes, I can't believe I'm getting engaged. *Aaaah!* And that, too, to a boy from London! So mysterious!

When Mama said there was an aunty who wanted to meet, I thought, Here we go again. I had exams going on, not that I care about them too much, but, well, I didn't want to fail my A-levels now. It would just be so embarrassing.

Anyway, I thought it was one of those *rishta* aunties who ask you if you know how to make tea and what you cook etc., but when I came out, with my hair kind of messy and not blow-dried, she was quite nice. She asked me about my studies and what I'd like to be. She mentioned she had a daughter too and I noticed her eyes tear up as she said this. My heart kind of broke a little for her.

Then she mentioned that her son had left for London right after she lost her daughter and he lost his sister. I have a little

161

sister too; I don't know how I would deal with such a loss. *Uff*, it's too much to even think about. To lose a sibling and be all alone in a foreign country must have been horrible. And then I was shown a picture—oh my God, he was gorgeous. If I were to marry this guy, it would blow my friends' minds! I knew they would be so jealous. Their crushes are always celebrities, but, this guy, he was just something. I wondered if he played a musical instrument—that would be so hot.

I sat with Aunty Faiza and politely answered some more of her questions. I also showed interest in whatever the ladies were talking about, while I imagined all the things that needed to be done before this Zohaib was to meet me for the first time. Aunty already gave me his number, so that we could have a chat sometime.

Since he's been here, though, it's been a little odd. He is jittery and nervous and unsure. I'm still figuring out if he's even listening when I'm talking to him. I try to keep the conversation going, while he either distractedly keeps checking his phone or completely zones out. I thought I looked pretty, and the earrings I wore were my favourite. I even googled "loss of a sibling" before coming out today. Obviously, I wasn't going to talk about it or anything—that would be stupid, especially because we're not even comfortable around each other yet—but I want to understand where he is coming from. Aunty Faiza has said I shouldn't delve too much into the past with Zohaib, that she wants me to be a fresh and happy new start for him. I want to be that for him too. I do want people to see us together, though; I so wanted to post a picture of us today, but I felt awkward asking him. All in good time. He just seems the very intense type, if only he would speak to me.

My best friend, Zoya, says he looks like Zayn Malik. He actually does a bit, only with curly hair. She wants to meet him too, but, for now, I want to keep him to myself. Zoya says I'm so pretty, he'd be a fool not to like me. I told her to calm down and let me take a day at a time.

When Aunty asked me what I'd like to be, I didn't really take it seriously. But, for now, Aunty, what I'd like to be is…interesting enough to catch your son's attention.

NADIA

Karachi, Pakistan

"Nono, will you come to my nana's house with me? He's got a swimming pool!" Misha had said to me one day. "He's very rich, you know," she said, knowing exactly the effect this would have on me.

I never liked when she spoke about money, that obvious marker of our difference, the place where our two worlds departed absolutely: mine lined with defeat, aggression, quarrelling; hers with laughter, naivety, and swimming pools.

I agreed to go. Amma was not happy about it; she thought that I'd become too "modern" if I accompanied Misha on too many of her excursions: her nana's place, meeting her friends— oh, and the club where we pretended to be sisters. She didn't agree with the education I was getting; she thought it would ruin my chances of one day becoming a good wife. She was right and she was wrong.

That day, Misha won again, like she often did with me. But I always put on an excellent scowl and trudged along, dragging my feet, making a show of how I was doing Misha a favour. I didn't want her to think I was *dying* to go. Especially since Zohaib would also not be home; only Barey *sahab* stayed back on Saturdays. The rest of the family went to Nana's.

We packed into the car, Zohaib in the front seat and the three of us, Bari *baji*, Misha and me in the back. In my two years in Karachi, I had never been taken to Nana's house. Misha had asked for Amma's permission many times, but Amma always kept me back, telling her she needed me for something. This was a big moment, an inclusion. I was tremendously excited to see the big swimming pool and the mulberry tree Zohaib often mentioned. Nana's house was in the new part of Defence. He had only one neighbour, according to Misha: the neighbour whose tree the children shamelessly climbed to collect mulberries.

We sped along, stopping at traffic signals, saying "*Maaf karo*" to the beggars tapping on the window. A man was selling dried coconut; my stomach growled a little, looking at the water-laden tray. I quickly coughed to drown my stomach's calling. The car went along Shahrah-e-Faisal, and I began imagining myself in a swimsuit—the black one, with the strap around the neck—the one that the pretty woman on TV wears. I think her name is Meera, or is it Veena? Soon, I would be leisurely sitting by the pool. I had seen a pool before, of course, at the club—never understood how the water was so blue.

I had been daydreaming so intensely about swimsuits and pools, I was taken by surprise when the car stopped with a jerk. We had reached the bespoke dwelling, and the landscape was a sight to behold. It was stunning: a white mansion with tall glass windows, pillars, lavish trees both outside and inside the house. The gate was brown, strewn in gold, bejewelled with intricate carvings. I really thought it was made from real gold, back then. It was a large gate, with two cuboid pillar lights on either side.

The house looked at least twice as big as Misha's, and at least a hundred times the size of our house, back in Okara.

I rubbed my eyes to see if I could get a clearer picture. I wanted to seal this memory; it felt like I was there to meet the king.

That day, as I tumbled out of the car, my eyes fell not on the coveted mulberry tree, but on the majestic fountain that was in the middle of the courtyard. Water was gushing out of the mouth of a stone lion. It felt like I was in a dream. As I was admiring the fountain, Misha and Zohaib ran in, leaving me and Bari *baji* behind. She instructed me to go and sit in the kitchen, and called on the maid to show me the way. I quietly obliged, thinking perhaps Misha would come and get me from there and we could climb the mulberry tree to collect some of its famed juicy fruits to take back home. Her nana, or my *barey-barey sahab* wouldn't mind, I was sure. It wasn't even his tree; it was his neighbour's! As I sat in the kitchen, dreaming the dreams I often dreamed, another girl who was required to stay in the kitchen began speaking to me.

"I'm Saleeka. Who are you?" she asked me, looking at me strangely. I guess she couldn't quite place me, and was probably wondering why I was sitting with her and not with the children of the household, and why I was dressed in a frock. I almost regretted not wearing *shalwar kameez*. At least I would have fitted in somewhere.

"I'm Nadia," I said, too embarrassed to give more information.

I was served lunch in the kitchen too. I could hear voices from the garden; I stepped out in search of the children. Misha's cousins were there—lots of them. I walked around, looking for an exit, when I almost bumped into someone who could only have been Barey-barey *sahab*.

"*Aye*, girl, go! *Shoo!* You have no business being here." His tone was harsh. He didn't know who I was, but he shooed me away, anyway.

I ran back to the kitchen, scared and dejected. I sat on a stool, alone, for the rest of the evening. Misha had forgotten me. It was normal for her to do that sometimes, thinking only about herself. I sat there, fuming, my cheeks burning with humiliation. What had I been thinking? That I would be welcomed with flower garlands? Drums beating? I should have known my place. I should have avoided this shame. I vowed never to go to Nana's house again. I should listen to Amma more, I thought.

The gate I stood before this morning was the same brown-and-gold gate that I was in awe of all those years ago. The reason I had not wanted to go inside was because I didn't want to break that promise I had made to myself as a dejected child.

Barey-barey *sahab*'s house has lots of neighbours now, on each side. I tried to excuse myself, but I was compelled by Gulshan to go inside. I felt defeated by the prospect of narrating everything to her that happened so long ago. Besides, I was sure nobody would recognise me, all these years later, with this belly and the obvious weight gain. Who was to say another family didn't live here now, anyway? I guess I was wrong.

GULSHAN

Nadia has been dreadfully quiet since we returned home. First, she didn't want to go inside my new client's house. I couldn't just leave her outside, after such a long journey. Then, she wouldn't speak to me about it. She kept tugging her hair behind her ear, then biting her nails. Clutching her stomach. She remained far away from the new *baji*—Faiqa, her name was. Or was it Faiza? Even the *baji* was looking weirdly at her, casting her sideways glances. Or maybe she was just curious about Nadia's pregnancy—older women are always so inquisitive about younger pregnant women. Oh, but their house is just beautiful! A little dated, but still so grand. It has a fountain with a lion's face spilling out water. Imagine! It's really something. The garden is so big, it looks like a cricket stadium. They even have a huge swimming pool—I just wanted to jump right in! What do these people even do to earn that kind of money? I shake my head.

"Did you see that fountain? *Uff*, who thinks of such stuff?" I try to make conversation.

"Hmm," Nadia responds. Lying on her back, she's pretending to be asleep, but I can see her feet fidgeting. She's restless.

"And that pool—I so wanted to see it from the inside. Come to think of it, what would they even do if we actually took a plunge? Would they force two women out of the pool? Crime committed: swimming!" I announce like a news anchor, laughing at my own joke.

Nothing.

"Nado? Come on, what happened? Do you know *baji*? Why was she looking at you like that? Have you met her before?"

Nadia doesn't respond.

"*Acha*, are you making that *gajar ka bharta*? I could never figure out the recipe!"

Nadia is just completely unresponsive, at this point.

"Hello? What are we eating?" I continue, trying to figure out what's happening.

Her foot stops moving. I edge closer to the *charpoy* she is lying flat on. Her eyes are shut tight—too tight for her to actually be asleep. I touch her forehead. She flinches. I sigh.

I move towards the kitchen counter and grab two onions from the plastic container I've set up for vegetables. Next, I take some wheat flour and pour about a cup onto a flat metal dish. I mix some tap water and start kneading. I will just make *roti* for Nadia and myself. I turn the flame on, set up the pan so it heats up by the time my roti is rolled into a perfect circle. It won't be fun having dinner alone, but it looks like I don't have a choice. I hum a tune under my breath and carefully remove the pan once I am done. I sprinkle some salt and red chilli on some chopped onions and sit cross-legged on the *dari*.

At least I got a big order from the visit. Four fancy suits for the maids—I think they have some big function coming up. I will have to work late into the night, if I am to get them stitched in time. I could've used the help with the work, but Nadia seems to have retreated into her own world. No matter.

I finish my dinner and put away my plate. I'll just wash it in the morning with the breakfast dishes. I'd better get working. One last look at Nadia, and I head towards my sewing machine.

ZOHAIB

Karachi, Pakistan

Mama summons me to Nana's study, which is now her art studio. She started painting a few years ago, once her depression was under control. Her therapist suggested she engage in an activity that released the tension from her body. She chose painting, a passion long forgotten since becoming a mother.

In front of me is a large canvas painting, still incomplete. The typography is done with a pencil, but the lettering is not fully coloured in with paint yet. In beautiful sweeping calligraphy, it says the Arabic text, *Inna lillahi wa Inna ilayhe Raji'un,* "To Allah we belong and to Him we return," from the Holy Quran. A supplication uttered whenever one hears of death or loss.

The room is furnished in a rustic style; there is a cabinet and a study table, which is pushed to the side and holds several brushes and palettes. The wall beside the cabinet is a hall of fame: framed photographs of Nana with the army chief, another with the ex-prime minister, one of some award being presented to Nana. The wooden flooring has paint splatter all over it. I laugh to myself remembering we were never allowed inside Nana's "special room" for fear of spilling anything in his pristine study. My phone beeps: it's a message from Talha. A part of me is empty without him—a void I feel every day. I lock my phone and slide it into my trouser pocket, focusing on Mama. One thing at a time.

Mama sits on an armchair, borrowed from one of the other rooms, it seems. It is sky blue, a sharp contrast to the dark colours of Nana's study.

"Mama."

"*Beta*, hear me out first. It's…It's been a tough—" she clears her throat—"a tough time, as you know. A tough time for you, as well."

Yeah, I only completely lost myself, Mama, and I was just a child, but please go on…

"It was unfair of me. It was deeply unforgiving of me. I should've been there for you."

I can see tears threatening to fall from the corner of her eyes. Her face, once youthful, is now full of deep lines of all shapes and sizes. Her eyes have deep pockets, dark and unpleasant. She looks old and weary, much older than her years.

"Your father…we couldn't carry on. You see, we couldn't be reminded…of Misha every day. When I looked at you, I would see Misha. When I looked at him, I would see her." She tries to pull herself together. "But all that is in the past. I want you to start a new life with Sumbul. She is young. She will be good for you, a breath of fresh air."

"Mama, I-I agreed to the engagement plans. B-But I'm not so sure. She knows nothing about me. How do we know she will be able to handle being with me? It doesn't seem right that she should be expected to marry me without knowing…everything," I say, my heart beating fast. I don't want to upset her.

"*Beta*, it's hard for you to move forward, I understand that. And Sumbul knows about Misha passing. Just trust me, don't

172

resist anything right now. This is best for you. She will help you forget those things. You don't need to carry them forward with you. And, about your father—he has a right to meet you, to talk to you. I don't want to withhold you from him any longer. I know it's not right. I just needed some time to figure myself out, to readjust to everything. But I do think now you should speak to your baba before the engagement. He yearns to have you back in his life. He loves you very much," she says, tears rolling down her face.

"Mama, don't cry." I can feel my eyes welling up with tears too.

"Call him, *beta*. I know you've been wanting to. Invite him. Spend time with him," she says, her voice cracking.

"I will, Mama—don't cry, please, I can't see you crying. I called him once, I will call again. I'll go visit him. I want to meet him. I don't want to hide anymore. I'm tired, Mama, so tired." I hug her, resting my head on her bony shoulder. She feels so fragile. "I'm here, now. *Shhh*, don't cry. *Shhh*, I'm here," I whisper to her.

She gives me a squeeze, kisses my face, and then lets out a sigh. "Come on, now—we've got to get your fitting done. Let's not dwell on the past. There is happiness coming into our lives, a bright young woman." She smiles. "I'll call up the designer. I thought maybe go traditional, with a waistcoat—what do you say?" She tugs a strand of grey hair behind her ear and blows her nose with a tissue.

"Sure, we can do that. But I want to try calling Baba again. Maybe we can go meet him after?" I suggest.

"Yes, but, *beta*, you go without me. If you manage to get through to him, I'll drop you to his house. I think it will be better if the two of you get a chance to connect," she says, getting up and inattentively dipping her brushes in the cup of mucky water.

I join her at the study table and, together, in silence, we close any tubes of paint that are without lids. I clear the used tissues and wrappers of granola bars that Mama eats while she paints. I switch off the lights as we walk out of the room.

"Zohaib, there's one more thing. Remember Nono, Nadia? Masi's daughter? I have a terrible suspicion that it was her who came in yesterday with the new tailor I've hired...It looked awfully like her. Anyway, let me call the designer now, see if he's available," she says nonchalantly as she climbs up the stairs, leaving me baffled, staring after her.

NADIA

Oh God, oh God, oh Allah! It was her! I have been to Barey-barey *sahab*'s house only once, but that one time was enough to make that memory haunting and indelibly seared into my mind. Standing at that gate, I hoped against all odds that Barey-barey *sahab* had passed away and sold the house to someone else. Maybe the house would be completely refurbished into another home, no ghosts lingering in the building. But I never expected Bari *baji* to actually *be* there. To stare at me, to think *less* of me, as she always seemed to in the past. Lesser than her children, some kind of a charity case—her little feel-good venture.

Emaan kicks me in the earliest hours of the morning. Why am I naming her Emaan when I have lost my faith? What good is faith when the world is always unfaithful? When people are always treacherous, disloyal? Why am I bringing you into this world of deceit and heartlessness? No, Emaan does not suit her. I will have to name her something else. *Misha.* I will bring you into this world and make a better life for you. I will not let you be treated the way I was. You will not be anyone's servant. You will not be anyone's charity case. I will not let this world of "*bajis*" destroy your spirit the way mine was destroyed. Maybe if I had never come to Karachi, maybe if I had lived the simple life, I wouldn't be this damaged.

There were days Bari *baji* was suspicious of me. She would treat me with disdain. The summer when Abida disappeared, I felt completely helpless. I found no solace in the *chorun*, not even in the sour candy Misha used to save for me. I would sit on the veranda all day, not paying attention to homework like I had before. My friend Shakeela, at school, even remarked on my weight loss. I wasn't concentrating in class. Even Shah Zaman, the cook, took pity on me, and didn't ask me for massages anymore. That was a small relief.

In that state of overwhelming sadness, and with a sense of deep injustice in the world, I went into Bari *baji*'s room. It was a big room, elegantly set up with a mirrored cabinet, a settee, and a four-poster bed like the one in the book Misha liked, *The Princess and the Pea*. I used to love that story, and I loved the *nakhras* of the princess. I walked right into Bari *baji*'s room, didn't knock, didn't check if there was anyone in there. I picked up one of her jewellery boxes—so ornate, with red and green stones, it looked like a piece of jewellery itself. I carefully removed the lid. Inside were some glorious pieces: a watch, a few rings, and a gold bracelet. In an instant, I grabbed the bracelet and hid it in my underwear, hoping it wouldn't fall out.

She didn't notice it for at least three days after. On the fourth day, she finally realized it was missing, and she went ballistic. I remember that day like it happened yesterday. I had just come back from the school; the van driver had been exceptionally mean and dropped me off a few kilometres away from the house. I had to walk all the way to 55 Alhamra. As soon as I entered, I could hear a commotion. Bari *baji* was one of those silent types, who hardly ever expressed anger, but, when she did, it was terrifying. As I walked along the patio to the veranda, Amma was emptying her *sanduk* in which she kept all our belongings.

"*Baji*, by Allah, every grain of wheat be *haram* on me if I ever steal anything of yours. May death be upon me if I ever put my hands on anything that you have prohibited me from touching. May death be upon me!" she was saying, beating her chest.

I quickly went into the kitchen, put my school bag on the counter, and filled a glass of water for Amma. I felt guilty for having put her in that predicament. I rushed to her, only to have the glass pushed out of my hand by Bari *baji* in her anger and thrown across the veranda. Tiny pieces of glass shattered on the floor. Amma pulled me close to her. I looked Bari *baji* in the eye without blinking. I felt so much rage. I hadn't stolen the bracelet because I liked jewellery or so I could sell it. I had stolen it so she could feel loss—of not having everything, of a disruption in her immaculate little world. So that she, too, knew how it felt to have something she loved just disappear. I know she had nothing to do with Abida, but it was all so unfair. The van driver, the massages, the abandonment at Nana's, the uniform three sizes too big, the leftover food, the feeling of always being the *other*...

A sharp pain erupts on my side, a scream escapes my lips. It's too early for my delivery; I'm not due yet. I think I'm panicking. But the pain is unbearable.

"Goshi! *Aaaaaagh!* GOSHI! Wake up! There's something... Something is wrong. *Aaaagh!*" I try to bite into the blanket, so the scream doesn't wake up the entire locality.

"What? What? Okay, I'm up, I'm up. Wait—let me get some money. Do you have money? We can go to the hospital. To the doctor." She is trying hard not to sound distraught.

The pain is not like a cramp. It's not coming and going. It's constantly piercing, like someone has decided to leave a hot coal in my body, and it's chewing up my insides.

"*Aaaagh!* I have...I have it in—" I take a deep breath— "in my purse," I say, not sure if I have enough. But somebody needs to do something about it. I can't—I can't stand it. I take a deep breath and let go. Misha, my Misha, swimming in my body. I'm drowning, she's drowning. I hear a faint thud, and everything goes black.

GULSHAN

Karachi, Pakistan

Being a woman in this country is not easy. Being a poor woman is a unique torment. When we are born, our mothers are told, with commiserations, "Don't worry, the next one will be a boy, God willing." We are ashamedly taken through life, being told to not attract attention, not to smile in case men get the wrong impression, but to smile so we look pretty for the guests; we're told to guard our body's secrets, to lie when we can't pray on account of our period, hide our sanitary pads; we must cover ourselves and, if someone still catcalls, we must bow our head, because apparently that's our fault too. Make a home, not a house, just *compromise*. Don't ask for too much, cross our legs always, lower our gaze. Cook well, clean, make a living but never announce it. Reproduce, but not for ourselves. Offspring—no bastards, please, not even from your legitimate husband whom you asked for a divorce.

I sit quietly, feeling Nadia's pain. Feeling her exhaustion. I, too, am a woman in this country.

The baby is fine, the doctor tells us. Stress-induced pain. Maybe rest for a week? Can we pay for the ultrasound?

Yes, we can.

Have we registered for the baby delivery with a doctor?

No, we haven't.

Would we be looking at hospitals where the bill will be covered?

Um…Would you be able to guide us?

Yes. There is Jinnah Post Medical and Indus Hospital that cover the charge. Would you like a recommendation?

Yes, please.

I hold Nadia's purse and hang it on my shoulder. My bag rests on my other shoulder. She looks weak. She looks tired. Her once bright and attractive personality is swollen and haggard. She has been through so much.

She is going through so much.

"Her name is Misha," Nadia tells me as we walk out of the hospital.

A family crowds a stretcher coming in, holding a man with a wound on his head. His clothes are dirty and there are blood stains on his white *shalwar kameez*. I avert my eyes.

"What?" I ask distractedly.

"Her name, the baby. She's not Emaan. Her name is Misha. I have lost my *emaan*," she says, pointing to her tousled hair, scoffing.

"Well, *emaan* is not just about covering your head. I mean, I cover mine, but it is more out of habit than religious preference. More for respectability than anything else. What you choose for yourself is entirely your choice. You will find your way. Your path will be what *you* want it to be. We find our *Rabb* in our hearts. Our own selves. To deny ourselves that is the biggest sin. You and I, we are lost souls. Dancing to the rhythm of others' expectations. The world is unforgiving. But we carry on, and our concept of belief keeps…evolving," I say, hesitant, concerned that I might upset her. "Who did you think of, back there, when you thought you were losing Emaan—I mean, Misha? Who did you beg for help?"

"Allah."

"Exactly! He is whom we return to in the most difficult moments of our life. Our *Rabb*," I say triumphantly.

"But people are so quick to judge, Goshi. Did you see the doctor's face when I hesitated before giving Mubashir's name? Like she had seen so many like me. Illegitimate, filthy, irreverent," she says scornfully.

"Yes, people judge. But we are better off here—in a big city, where nobody recalls anything from the day before. The reel of life changes every day. Karachi, the city of dreams and the city of heartbreak," I say, steering the conversation to lift Nadia's spirits.

The daylight is harsh, the heat pricking my skin. There are motorcyclists speeding by, some carrying entire families on the length of their seats. We strut along in our rickshaw, the engine sputtering. The seats are torn, a miniature Kaaba hanging from the rear-view mirror. The trees lining the streets are old and sparsely planted. The lights at the zebra crossing are broken. Every so often, the pot-holed road sends us jumping off our seats and the driver says, "*Bismillah*." Nadia holds on to her stomach; I hold on to Nadia. We are women of this decaying city. We are showpieces, we are badges of honour. Heaven lies at our feet, we are the backbone of this country, we are told. And yet, we are smashed, burned, slashed, shamed, wrecked, demeaned, broken, and discarded every single day.

ZOHAIB

Karachi, Pakistan

This time, Baba picks up on the second ring.

"Hello?"

"Baba, it's me…Zohaib," I say, as an afterthought.

"Of course, I recognise your voice, *beta*. I know you're here. I was waiting to hear from you," he says carefully.

I suspect he knows that Mama may have asked me to keep away. Baba has always been perceptive. He used to insist Mama was the pillar that kept everyone together, but I actually think it was Baba who was the foundation. He was always there with his wise, stabilising words, his silent presence sturdier than all of us combined.

"Can I come see you?"

"Yes. I'm home today. Wasn't feeling up to it, so I decided to work from home," he says. "You can stay with me…" He lets his words linger.

It's too soon to commit, I know, so I just agree to meet him at Alhamra—my childhood home, *our* childhood home. I remember playing cricket on my street. I remember Faisal from next door and Abdul from near the mosque. We would even get Shah Zaman to field, if we were short of players. Some days, boys from the club would also join us and we would discuss how to make the best *manja* for our kites and how to swing the cricket ball just enough so we could get the other person out. We would chalk out the pitch on the road. The cars would even slow down, on our street. They would never complain or speed; they knew this was our field.

We didn't need to play on the streets, though. Our house was grand enough that, if we wanted, we could just play in our garden. We had a gigantic garden; the grass was lush and abundant. The water was never from the tankers, like we get in Nana's house, in Defence; we never worried about not getting enough. The bougainvillea trees bloomed all year around, while the *cheeku* trees were more generous in the winter. Some evenings, we would roll tyres out of the garage and make them into posts to play a game we invented, called "kick ball." It was essentially baseball, with four bases, but, instead of a bat, we would kick. The house at 55 Alhamra was a house of joy. It was also the house where I lost Misha.

"See you in a few hours, Baba."

As comfortable as I am at Nana's, my best memories are at 55 Alhamra. I have memories with Misha and Nono, I have memories with Baba. Baba, coming over to give me one last kiss before bedtime. Baba, quizzing me on all the countries of the world and their capitals. Baba going out for his early morning walk, and me joining him. Some days, Misha would also tag along. But I didn't mind that. Baba never loved either of us more. He always had this way of making us both feel special.

I think of the many things Baba taught me. I think of the many things he *could* have taught me. He taught me how to fly

183

a kite, how to convert currency rates from American dollars to Pakistani rupees to pound sterling. He taught me how to do business, how to buy at a lower rate and sell at a higher price, and to never tell trade secrets to anyone. He taught me how to deliver a perfect bouncer in cricket and what a tiebreaker was in tennis. He taught me how to climb a tree and get the best fruit.

What he didn't teach me was how to love a woman or how to ask for help when I needed it. He never taught me how to communicate my feelings, how to shave my beard, how not to be disappointed when I fail a test or tank an interview. He never taught me how to keep believing when the entire world falls apart, and he never taught me how to forgive others and myself.

MASOOD HASHIM

Karachi, Pakistan

It's a homecoming, of sorts. My humble abode has felt much less like a home, in recent years, and more like a guest house. I have people who cook for me, a gardener who maintains the garden, a sweeper who cleans the drains. My room is cleared of dirt and my bed sheets are shaken fiercely every morning to remove any dust mites lingering on the surface. The curtains are drawn back, and the windows opened to let in fresh air. There is no unnecessary chatter, no bickering; no children making mistakes. A silent riot situating itself uncomfortably. The abundance of memories are only remnants of occupation—a life spent, but not really lived.

Zohaib and I have had conversations over the years, but we have hardly ever truly communicated. We have had lunches, but never really reminisced about the stomachful of recollections we both carry around. He has lived a substantial portion of his life deprived, unattended to. I have been the very father I hoped I would never become.

Losing one child led me to lose my entire family. They say loss comes in clusters.

Death is the most terrible of things, for it is the end, and nothing is thought to be either good or bad for the dead, Aristotle said, but what does it do to the living? How does one cope with grief that comes in waves? Ebbing and flowing, crashing, and disbanding.

One must learn to swim.

Zohaib is coming to see me. He sounds better than he has in years. Like a heavy cloud has lifted. I hope I can be inspired by him and make my fog disappear too.

The doorbell rings. Someone has answered it. I hear footsteps climbing the staircase.

"Baba!"

I get up, straighten out my *kurta*. His face is a little blurry; I shuffle to find my glasses. I want to see him clearly, every line, every curve.

I envelop him in a hug. He is leaner than he was before. His face rests on my shoulder, a new feeling. All these years of visiting him in London, I never had more than a side hug from him. I hold him close. He has not grown taller since I last saw him, but he has shaved. His hair is long, curling up at the front. He has pierced his left ear. Talha's influence, no doubt.

"*Beta*, my *bacha*," I say now, sniffling. I hadn't realised I was crying. There is a flow behind the deep pockets of my eyes. I remove my glasses to wipe them. He looks around for a tissue, takes one out of his pocket.

"Baba, I-I wanted to invite you t-to my engagement. I'm sorry I haven't been back before. Ma-Mama wasn't ready to let me…let me come yet. She doesn't mean to…" His voice trails off.

"I know, *beta*—it's all right. There is a time for everything," I say, lighting my cigarette as I ease into my leather chair. This habit has lured me into its claws, having avoided it most of my adult

186

life. It will slowly be the ruin of me, but what part of me is not already in ruins?

"Baba, I'm here. I don't want to go back. I th-think I'm ready to be back," he says tensely, as I gesture for him to take a seat next to me. My flesh, my blood feels alien in my new reality.

"Whatever you want. You can choose to do whatever you want, *bachey*; you are old enough, and, from what I see, well enough equipped. I let you be on your own for too long. For too long I hid behind my work. You needed me, my son—and I, you. I owe you an apology. Several, actually…" My voice breaks a little.

"No, Baba, you were grieving. We all were," he says, getting up, kneeling next to me. He takes my hand, on which the veins are now visible. It does not feel the way it used to when I would hold his little hand in my palm.

"No, let me say it, *bachey*. I should have been stronger. Your mother was inconsolable; she was slowly disappearing, dissolving in her grief. I should have kept you near me, my son. I should have protected you. I didn't—I didn't know how. Farrukh Uncle said London would be good for you, and I took the first solution suggested to me," I say.

I want to tell him I was suicidal. Many times, I imagined myself melting into my anguish. I imagined myself never waking up, drowning in my agony, holding my breath till I sputtered and coughed. I can't tell him that, though; it is not fair of me to think about myself only.

"I'm sorry," I say simply.

He is a man, my little boy. He has grown, and I vow to be there for him now. I know I have let too much time go. But, *Falling down is not failure. Failure comes when you stay where you have fallen*, my beloved Socrates says. And I will not stay there any longer.

NADIA

Karachi, Pakistan

I feel much better. I lie on my back; I hear water dripping from the taps, observe the spiderwebs on the window. This is my home, now. It wasn't like I had to sell anything to come here. I left the squalid home I had shared with Mubashir and found that everything I wanted to keep could easily fit in a single suitcase. When it was time to leave the hostel, it was easy to pack up again.

There are days I miss Mubashir. Now that I have distance and space from him, I can remember there were good days too. Like when I first accepted my job at the office, or when Mubashir was not wasting my hard-earned salary on his *nasha*. There were nights we would go on his bike for a cold Pepsi, or for *nan khatai* biscuits with a cup of *karak chai*, or boiled eggs with chickpeas. We would just drive around when the coldest spells hit the cultural capital. Me in a scarf and coat, and Mubashir in a light sweater. Mubashir never felt cold. We would drive by the Ichhra market, past the Gawalmandi, the food street, the minarets looming in the distance, the smog letting us only see the outlines. Lahore has a personality of its own.

188

Goshi is out delivering her orders. She says she will stop by the Jinnah Post Medical Hospital and the Indus Hospital to see if they will register me. I could have my baby at home, but, to be honest, I've experienced Karachi only as a child and have no other well-wishers here that could assist or support me. I stare at the cracked ceiling; there is a lizard in one corner of the room. I can hear its chirping, since the fan turned off. It stops and moves intermittently, as if stalking something, but there is nothing else I can see that could be the lizard's prey. It runs from one corner to the middle of the wall, right where it connects with the roof. I don't know how long I stare at It for, but then there is a clink, and the door handle is turned.

"You will not believe who just called!" says Gulshan. No greeting, no asking after me.

"Who?" I ask.

"Your Zohaib," she says dramatically.

"*My* Zohaib? What do you mean?" I say, although there haven't been any other Zohaibs in my life, so it has to be him, especially after my showing up at his nana's house.

"Come on. Prince Zohaib of the—" she pretends to speak like a royal soldier—"where was he the prince of again?" she asks, smirking.

"He wasn't the prince of anywhere. He's probably married with three kids, driving a Ferrari, and showing off his *gori* wife," I say spitefully. I don't know where all that came from.

"Well, if he has all that, why is he calling me to see if I have any way of contacting you? Oh, yes! I do!" She does a little dance. She has a black plastic bag in her hand, so the dance looks extremely awkward, but she does it anyway.

"*Uff*, you monkey," I say, trying to turn on my side. My back hurts. "What did he want? Also, did you end up going to the

189

hospital?" I ask, remembering she had promised me that. It wasn't going to be long, now.

"Well, he wanted to meet you, asked if it's okay to meet at Nisar Shaheed Park tomorrow," she says, snapping her fingers.

"Goshi, I don't think I can deal with this right now. You know, I have thought about so many scenarios in my head over the years, if I ever did meet him. And maybe some part of me wanted to, but I have lived through so much pain from that family…"

"I know, Nado, but coming back to Karachi is a clean slate for you, a new life. Let's see what he has to say for himself," she says.

"I just don't know. These parks also give me the creeps. The people there will stare at my large belly," I say, more concerned about what Zohaib would think if he saw me now.

"Well, there is nothing unnatural about a pregnant woman going for a walk. Oh, and, yes, I went to Indus, and they said they do cover it, but if it's more than one night we will have to pay for the room." She places her plastic bag on the counter. "Also! Ghazala *baji* finally paid up, so we are going out to have *kulfi*!" she says in a sing-song voice.

Her energy is infectious. I could lie here all day and be gloomy, or I could get up, go out with her and have a *kulfi*. Option B, madam! I will get out of this mood, this dread that I have been feeling ever since we visited Barey-barey *sahab*'s house.

"So, I'm thinking I will WhatsApp Zohaib that we are coming," she says, trying to sound casual.

"Er, I never said I would go, Goshi." I look at her, narrowing my eyes.

"Come on! What's the worst that could happen? He's a total jerk and we walk away? They don't get clothes stitched from me? Big deal! I have so many clients! Remember, we don't work for them; we can leave any time we want," Goshi continues.

190

"Okay," I say, my heart pounding as if it will jump out of my chest.

"Okay? Really?" Goshi says disbelievingly.

"Well, you make a good case, madam," I say.

"Yes, I do!" she exclaims.

I don't know what he wants or what he will think of me being pregnant without a husband. It had to be now, after all these years. I would have carried on with my life without any shade of my past tinting my present. But maybe there is more to this, me ending up back in Karachi.

"Let's go have that kulfi," I say, as I pull myself up from the *charpoy*.

ZOHAIB

Karachi, Pakistan

"So, you'll call me?" Sumbul asks me, fluttering her lashes. She has this habit of blinking rapidly. I think the lashes are not real, but I dare not ask her. I don't know how to tactfully bring up women's beauty treatments here—or anywhere, for that matter.

"Yes, sure," I say. I never call. I don't know what to talk to her about. The good thing is she does most of the talking.

"See you," she says, and plants a light kiss on my cheek. I'm startled by this display of affection, and almost feel bad about not connecting with her. She's really trying.

"Thanks," I say stupidly.

She leaves the car and walks over to the gate, turning momentarily to wave at me. I wave back and drive off before the gate opens.

I haven't told her what my "commitment" is. She doesn't press me. I don't think I'm ready to share my complicated past with her yet.

I'm on my way to meet Nadia and her cousin, Gulshan, but hopefully just Nadia. After Mama revealed that she thought

Nadia had accompanied the new tailor she's hired, I snuck Mama's phone from her room while she showered and went through her contacts to find the tailor's number. I was so nervous calling her, afraid that I was making a huge mistake, but now, here I am, suddenly on my way to see Nadia again, after all these years. I wonder what she looks like. Will she remember our friendship? I grip the steering wheel tighter on account of my sweaty palms.

I drive past the commercial avenue, Zamzama, which used to be the high-fashion shopping street. The night before Eid, no one could find parking and Baba would have to park streets away. We would walk through the narrow alleys to visit the shops, which were buzzing with chatter, decorated with gleaming lights. Now, most of the shops had shifted to the Dolmen Mall, a multi-storey, multi-brand mall, just up ahead.

Would it be embarrassing, seeing each other after so long? Would it be devastating? I don't think I can handle being devastated. I have half a mind not to drive towards the park; maybe this Pandora's box should be left unopened. No, she will be on her way too, now. I push these thoughts away. Although, I don't quite know why I want to meet her. To apologize? To be apologized to? What exactly am I looking for? She could be very angry. Heat rises to my cheeks with that thought. What am I here to fix?

I pull up near the entrance and pay for the ticket. Although it's just ten rupees, it strikes me as a little odd that one should pay to go to a public park. But the park is beautiful. A sandy path meanders through it. Lots of people are out walking, some jogging. There are several enclosures with gorgeous flowers and other ornamentation. The path is also lined with plants, including dog flowers and jasmine all the way round. I walk along, wondering how I am to figure out where the two women will be. There was no specific place we decided to meet at. I find myself enjoying the stroll.

I see a man standing by a bench. Two women are busy biting into baked corn, while talking to the tall man. Could it be her? One of them looks a bit older—in her fifties—while the other could easily be Nadia's age. I am edging closer, unsure if I should approach them, when the younger one suddenly looks up and makes eye contact. She is wearing hoop earrings and a sparkly nose pin. Nope, definitely not Nadia.

I pick up my phone to dial Gulshan's number. There is no point in looking around; it is a gigantic park. Better to just call and ask where they are.

It rings three times before she picks up.

"Hello?" she says.

"Hello! I'm here. Zohaib. Can you tell me where I can find you both?"

"Oh, by the gate. Wait—which number is this?" she asks someone, maybe Nadia.

"Yes, gate three. Come near the benches where the swings are, yes? Come," she says.

I look around to see which gate I'm at. There is no gate nearby. I walk along the path till I see a gate in the periphery of my vision. Gate one, it says. I keep walking.

After half a kilometre of walking, I reach gate three. I see the benches. And I see her. Unmistakably, unquestionably her.

I walk closer and I remember her sitting on the veranda, her eyes sparkling, her mouth grinning. Her climbing the *cheeku* tree. Her on the roof.

"H-Hi," I say.

194

NADIA

Karachi, Pakistan

"Hello," Goshi says.

I stay quiet. I fidget with the shawl I decided to wear last minute to cover my belly. This is not the first thing I want him to see of me.

"I'm going to go for a walk," Goshi says, and gets up.

"M-May I sit?" Zohaib asks.

He is handsome. He has a beautiful jawline, brown hair curling over his forehead. His hair sways dramatically under the light breeze. I resist the urge to reach out and put it behind his ear so I can see his eyes clearly.

"Yes, sure," I squeak.

"I-I've just come back to Karachi. I w-was in London. I would've found you earlier," he says.

I don't know what I'm feeling. Yes, if you had found me earlier, I wouldn't have married Mubashir. I would've pursued a different career; I would have got help from you. If you'd had a backbone, you would've stopped your mother from accusing me. But I don't say anything.

"I'm sorry. I blame myself. I should've..." His voice trails off.

I shift and my shawl slides off.

"Oh," he says, looking at my stomach.

His reaction makes me defensive. "What?" I say to him sharply. "You haven't seen a pregnant woman before?" I know I have this anger, this fury inside of me. It comes and goes. It's almost like I forget it exists and then it returns with a vengeance. I am not myself; I become this rage.

I don't want to be angry at him. Oh, Zohaib, you were just a child too, and you were always so good to me. I don't mean what I'm saying, but I can't help it. I will myself to be quiet, but it's not in my control.

"What did you expect, coming here? What did your family think of what they did to me? Huh? That you all managed to pull me out of my poverty? In that godforsaken house? You all thought you could treat me like your pitiful charity case? And then just shove me out whenever convenient!" I can't stop myself now. "All of you! You deserved it! For what all of you did! *She* deserved it!" I say. I put a hand on my mouth. No. No. No. NO.

What am I saying? What have I said? The remorse is instant.

His eyes widen with disbelief.

I didn't mean to. *I didn't mean to say that.* Words protect hearts. Mine just did the opposite.

"Y-You're not who I thought you would be," he says quietly. He opens his mouth to say something else, but closes it again. He gets up, looks back at me with a slight shake of his head, as if to clear it.

Misha kicks me hard; I bite my lip. My heart splits in half—nothing likes to be split like that.

In another life, I would've been more eloquent. In another life, I would've made better decisions. I didn't mean to do all that I did; I didn't mean to say all that I said.

"Don't go," I whisper into the air.

GULSHAN

Karachi, Pakistan

I walk along the circumference of the park, observing all kinds of people. A park is where you see pretty much everything. This girl wearing running tights, headphones connected to her phone on her arm, jogging at a steady fast speed. This hundred-year-old man being walked around by another, younger, man—no doubt a walk prescribed by the doctor. A young couple, off the beaten path, somewhere in the shadows, doing hanky-panky. Women in their track pants, in twos and threes, chatting on their evening walk. Children playing, running, climbing. Rich, middle class, poor. There are carts near the gate serving a range of snacks— warm fries, candyfloss, chickpeas in newspapers—and small bubble wands for the children. The evening is pleasant, the sun dipping in the sky, its brightness dimming as minutes pass. A throng of mosquitoes zooms by. I see three bearded men crossing the park, heading towards the mosque entrance from within the park as *Maghreb* draws near. I wonder if they are required to pay for the ticket just to cross through the park. I also wonder what Nadia and Zohaib are up to.

We don't get fairy tales. Our marriages are not what we see on TV. If we fall in love, we do it with the wrong person. If our marriage is decided, the burden of dowry is upon our parents. If we fight with our husbands or in-laws, our sisters get sent home too, because they are also married into the same family. Our marriages are a way to have daughters leave, so there's one less person to feed. I had a different life. My mother passed away when I was days old. When Bua took me in, I was just a baby. She was the only mother I knew.

I had hoped Nadia would get the fairy tale, prove our lives were not cursed. Sometimes, I lived through her experiences. "Oh, you're studying!" I'd say. She would talk so smart sometimes. All these things I could never imagine. She taught us new games—games no one in our village knew.

Things didn't happen for her as I had hoped; maybe life was giving her a second chance?

I look at my phone to check the time; I think I've given them long enough. I shouldn't leave her alone too long, in her condition. I walk back the same way I came. If they are still talking, I will just hang back, but I need to be around her. I know there is barely an age gap between us, but, since she hurtled back into my life and home, I feel protective towards her.

I find her on the same bench. She's on her own, her head is bent, and she is clutching her belly and—wait—*crying*?

What did Zohaib do? I should never have set this up. In my heart, I felt maybe, just maybe, this meeting would lead to something good for Nadia—but here she is weeping.

"*Aray*, what happened?" I ask her as I draw closer to the bench.

"Nothing," she says, sniffing. Her face is pale, and her eyes are bloodshot. She is making an effort to appear unaffected.

"It's okay. Let's go. It was a mistake, all of it—my fault. I should never have answered the phone. Typical entitled spoilt brat, this one," I say, as I spit my 7UP into the grass.

"No, it's my fault. I said things I should never have spoken," she says softly. "I don't know if my punishment is over."

"What did you say? What are you talking about? Don't say such ridiculous things," I say, frowning.

"Goshi, my *Rabb* is not happy with me," she says, almost inaudibly.

"Don't be a fool. Come, let's go back home. You must be tired. I just need to drop their clothes for the engagement function tomorrow and I will never take an order from these people again, *bas*—they can find themselves another tailor," I say indignantly.

"He's not happy. He's not happy, my *Rabb*," she mumbles.

I look at her to see who she's talking to, but she seems to be in her own thoughts. I take her hand and we silently walk towards the park gate.

ZOHAIB

Karachi, Pakistan

I look sideways at Sumbul as she adjusts the diamond necklace resting on her collarbones. The jewels sparkle under the spotlights that are directed at us; her face is illuminated under all that shiny make-up, done professionally. She looks stunning.

Baba smiles at me from the crowd. He's donning a tailored *kurta pyjama* and a waistcoat. His salt-and-pepper hair is visible under his Jinnah cap. He looks happy. Mama is entertaining the guests, whizzing from one corner to the other, sometimes with a tray of sweets, other times hopping onto the stage to fix Sumbul's dupatta. She hasn't looked like this in a long time. I have been unsure about this for a while, but, looking at my parents, I feel I owe it to them to at least give this a sincere chance, and I feel an optimism blossoming within me too. Perhaps Mama was right all along.

The other evening was equal parts embarrassing and terrible. I don't know what I had been expecting. Perhaps I wanted validation, some kind of comfort in knowing that it's okay to move on. Maybe even a little support, friendship, *love*? I had hoped I could make things better. But some things can't be fixed, especially if you had a part to play in breaking them.

Life is metaphorically funny, literally cruel. We take things for granted when we have them, and yearn for things that seem most complicated. I lost a part of me the night Misha died, and my life changed forever. For a long time, I replayed the scene in my mind, going over the day again and again, trying different things, taking different actions. I replayed it so much that I don't know now what exactly happened. I played around with reality and what could have been. Mama and Baba would still be together. I would have lived here all my childhood. I would have been a different person. Misha would still be here, a young woman now.

"Hey, are you okay?" Sumbul brings me back to the present.

"Yes, just g-got lost in my thoughts for a moment there," I say.

She points to the camera, and I smile dutifully.

The stage is beautifully set in dazzling mirrors and flower arrangements. Tall candle stands are displayed atop white, intricately carved tables. Sumbul and I sit on a sofa in the middle, like royalty. There is a photographer clicking away pictures of us and the two families, and a videographer who is filming the entire event. I'm sure this video will only be seen once, to spot everyone, and then placed in a drawer.

"Hey, do you want to go get coffee, after all this is over?" Sumbul says to me, hesitatingly. She looks at ease being the centre of attention. It's a role she is perfectly suited to. But there is concern in her eyes, an awareness that beyond the wedding day lies a lifetime of marriage.

It's possible I haven't given her enough credit. Yes, she's younger than me. Yes, she doesn't know much about me, except that I have lived in London and lost a sister. She doesn't know how I have struggled, how I continue to struggle with anxiety. She doesn't know what medication I need to sleep at night. But, for the first time in years, I feel like I am ready for a fresh start. She may not know me, but nothing will change unless I *let* her know *me*.

Look, observe.

Maybe I have been too quick to write Sumbul off. Maybe I have been too quick to blame myself for everything that happened. I wouldn't say everything happens for a reason, because, by God, I can't understand why some people are taken away before their time. Or maybe I don't understand that it *was* their time to go. I don't know. I don't know. I can't question what has already happened, and too much has happened. The only thing now is to move forward and to allow myself to find happiness in places I didn't expect to find it. Observe the people around me, find who needs me, and how. And maybe, just maybe, look for someone *I* need.

"Yes, yes, Sumbul, I would like that," I say, turning my face and displaying another smile for the camera.

NADIA

I wake up in the middle of the night, sweating. My forehead is burning up and my stomach is in a spasm, due to the pain. The cramps aren't like anything I have ever experienced before. I sit up and fold over. I feel dizzy and nauseous.

"Goshi," I whisper. I can't seem to find my voice. My head is spinning. My throat feels like it has turned into lead; I find swallowing a chore.

"Goshi," I say, a little louder. The cramp comes again—this time, I dig my nails into my skin. I know it's time. This must be what the doctor said contractions would feel like.

"Goshi! Wake up!" I scream this time.

"What? What?" she exclaims.

"We need to go to the hospital. I think...I think she's coming. Misha is coming!" I say.

We have nothing prepared. The only thing I have is this romper I picked up in Lahore when I found out I was pregnant.

My mind flashes back to Okara, to the fields, the okan trees, Abida.

203

"Goshi, call Abida. Tell her the baby is coming. Oh, tell her, please. I don't know…I don't know what I'll do," I cry in pain.

Goshi is scrambling. She's tripped over something in the dark, and now she is gathering up the sheets.

"What are you doing?!" I ask.

"Won't we need sheets?" she asks, panicked.

"*No!* We need to go now! Unless *you* want to deliver her here?" I look at her panicked face.

"No, no. Okay. Will we need an ambulance? How will we go?" she asks, confused.

"No, I can…I can walk. Go fetch the cash. *Aaah!*" I say, as another contraction flows through my body. "Go take out whatever money I have left in the envelope. Everything. We might need it," I say, my mind suddenly alert.

I never thought I would have to do this without Amma. Without Mubashir. But life has written it for me. I don't know how I will manage my life. I don't have the capacity to manage myself, let alone a baby. But she is coming, and I must be *ready*.

ZOHAIB

"Can we quickly just stop by my house?" Sumbul asks, puffing her cheeks. "These clothes are too uncomfortable. Not to mention, this jewellery needs to go into Mama's safe!"

We have left Nana's house and, as promised, I'm taking Sumbul out for coffee. The event was beautifully put together by Mama and Sumbul's parents. Mama decided to host it at Nana's house because it has a bigger garden. If Sumbul has to change her clothes, we'll have to drive all the way to Korangi. Okay, not Korangi, but Khyban-e-Saadi is literally the edge of the Defence Housing Authority. Such a detour.

"Okay," I say, looking at the time on the car dashboard. I am exhausted. Four hours of smiling for the guests and camera has given me a headache. But I know it's not wise to drive around with bridal jewellery on the roads of Karachi, so I agree.

I enjoy driving on these streets. This part of town is wonderfully developed compared to the rest of Karachi. The roads have signs, the traffic signals are functional, and there is even a bit of greenery at the sides of the roads.

We stop outside Sumbul's house, and she quickly rushes inside in her high heels. A few minutes later, she is back, wearing her jeans and flat pumps, comfortable and ready for getting a coffee. I decide I like her better like this. She taps on my window.

"Hey, can I drive?" she asks sweetly, her eyes sparkling.

I don't mind being driven around, but I'm not sure she has a licence.

My doubt must show, because Sumbul says, "Come on, I'm old enough. Trust me, I've attended driving school!"

I'm sold. I pull the door handle, step out, and let her in. She adjusts the seat and rear-view mirror, and we both click on our seat belts.

"So, since I'm the local here, should we try some new places? Verde or New Castle Café? I've heard great things about their tarts. My God, I'm suddenly so hungry! I didn't even have a proper dinner, with everyone staring! Plus, I was too scared I would eat away all my lipstick!" she chuckles.

I'd had no qualms about eating, of course. The catering service had set up a tantalizing table with a variety of Chinese dishes Mama had selected. The meal was followed by crunch ice cream from Peshawari, and crème brûlée from another renowned eatery.

"Sure, you decide," I say to her.

She starts the engine and swerves the car into a U-turn; her street leads to a dead end.

"I was thinking that maybe, now that everything is official, we can, you know, get to know each other a little bit more," she says to me cautiously.

"Yes. Well, I'm an introvert, as you can see. I-I've struggled with, um, things f-from the past," I say.

"Yes, I know, and I don't, by any means, want to pressure you into anything," she says.

We are now on the main Ittehad road, and, even though Sumbul has good control of the car, I'm a little uncomfortable with her speed.

We stop at a signal. There is tapping on the door.

"May your *jori* be eternally together," says the little boy, in Urdu.

Seeing Sumbul driving, he switches to English—"Don't break my heart, *baji*—"and thrusts flowers at us through the open window.

Sumbul excuses herself from the boy and shuts the window. The little boy is so young, my heart sinks for him; I gesture for him to come to the window on my side. The traffic signal turns green and Sumbul speeds past the boy.

"Hey, I wanted to give him something," I say.

"Oh! But you don't know what gangs they belong to," she says. "Most of these little boys have to report to their master, Mama told me; money you give them doesn't really go to their families," she explains. She is looking at me sideways.

"Aren't you supposed to turn from here? "I point to a *khyban* on the left.

"Oh!" Sumbul says, and breaks abruptly, simultaneously turning the car. The tyres protest and skid on the road. The car feels like it's out of her control.

"Sumbul! Watch out!" I scream.

There is a loud thud and a bang as the car hits something. I hold on to the dashboard, but there is a second collision. My head is hurting and so is my shoulder. I'm screaming, but I can't hear myself.

"Sumbul!" I say, but no voice emerges.

The car finally comes to a halt somewhere. There is shattered glass all over me. The windscreen must have broken. My face is hurting. There is a siren. Is it the police? An ambulance? How did it get here so quickly? Is Sumbul okay? Am I okay? I try to open one eye, but I can't seem to.

I try to wriggle free from my seat belt.

"Sumbul!" This time, the voice comes out.

"Yes," she says meekly.

Thank God she's alive. Thank you, thank you, Allah. Thank you.

As far as I know, I am too. But what did we hit?

GULSHAN

I am scared, to be honest. Nadia seems to be taking this well. I don't think she can walk. I take out my phone and call the number I have memorised for a Chhipa Ambulance. I don't think taking a rickshaw is the best option, right now.

Nadia's face is pale. Not glowing or beautiful anymore. Ghostly white. She is not saying much, but I can tell how much pain she is in. I slowly guide her down the stairs, holding a shoulder bag with her essentials. I have locked the door behind me; I don't know how long this is going to take. But this is what I signed up for, to do this with her and for her.

I tried calling Abida *bajjo* when Nadia told me to, but she didn't pick up and I didn't have time to call her back. This one's on me. I hope the ambulance arrives soon. I can't take this responsibility alone. Will we be charged? Oh, *Rabb*, please help us and let us reach the hospital safely.

"*Aahhh!*" Nadia says softly. She is holding her stomach, as if to protect the baby from falling out.

We stand at the *chorangi*, from where I have already instructed the ambulance to pick us up. It should be here soon. *Just five more minutes*, I say to Nadia silently.

She's a warrior, my Nadia. This is one more battle she is going to win, I'm sure. The road is quiet; most vendors have closed shop. It's a starless night, as most nights in Karachi are. The air is suddenly chilly; I should wrap Nadia in a shawl or a sheet, but it's too late to go back now. I'm praying the ambulance comes soon. What if her water breaks while we are still waiting? I don't even know what to expect. Will she let out a scream, followed by a sudden gush of fluid, like in the films? What will we do then? Nothing will happen. Just do *tasbih*. "*Astaghfirullah! Astaghfirullah!*" I recite on imaginary prayer beads.

I can hear the siren from far away. Okay, it's here, it's here. The ambulance slows down in front of us. It is an old vehicle, dilapidated from use. I don't complain; it's going to save baby Misha. I will be forever grateful for Driver *chacha*, forever grateful, I'm saying. There is a paramedic who is helping Nadia in. He's taking her blood pressure.

She's strapped in. I'm sitting on a foldable seat beside her. Driver *chacha* is back in the driver's seat. He says we will reach Indus Hospital in twenty minutes.

"*Aaaahh! Owwwwww!*" Nadia moans every few minutes. She's not screaming, but I know she wants to. She is having trouble breathing.

I wave at the paramedic, but he is on his phone.

"Bhai, can you put an oxygen mask on her, or something? Is she going to faint?" I say, flustered by her obvious discomfort.

"Calm down, sister; we will have all the equipment at the hospital," he says.

We're passing through the streets of Karachi. A city of crime and chaos, under the florescent glow of the streetlights it almost looks ethereal. There are few cars on the road. The ambulance is taking the liberty to speed. I stumble sideways as we make a turn.

It will all be okay, I tell myself. Misha will be out in no time. And then we can—

Crash.

The ambulance collides into something metal—another vehicle. I feel dizzy as it drifts, and there's another jolt when it crashes into something else. I've slid off the edge of my seat. My arm is hurting. My head is throbbing. Someone is screaming. Oh *Rabb*, oh *Rabb*, oh *Rabb*, what did you do?

I'm trying to detach myself from the seat belt I had been asked to wear earlier. There is a sharp pain shooting up my wrist into my elbow. I may have broken it.

Oh! Nadia! Misha!

Please, Allah. Please, *astagfirullah, ya Rabbi!* Let them be okay, please let them be okay, I pray, as tears of pain and fear leak from my eyes.

ZOHAIB

Karachi, Pakistan

I have some minor bruising and a trauma to the head. Sumbul has fractured her rib and may need eye surgery. Some shards of glass went into her cornea, causing a slight tear. The events of the past three hours have left me dumbfounded.

We got into an accident with an ambulance.

I should never have let Sumbul drive. We shouldn't have gone out for coffee after such an exhausting night. We should not have gone on that road. I shouldn't have told her to turn at such short notice. I shouldn't…Oh, Lord.

If this was not crazy enough…I don't know if I should laugh or cry, at this point. It seems all too surreal. Out of a horror movie.

Nadia was in the ambulance.

It seemed like God was playing a twisted joke with me. How on earth!

The ambulance was in a bad way. Thankfully, the paramedic was able to call for backup and another one had quickly arrived, bringing us all here. For a second, there, I thought I was losing everything, yet again. Two life-ending moments, both with Nadia in them. Fate has such a terrible sense of humour.

I want to go check on Sumbul. I want to go check on Nadia. But I sit, stupidly, on the chair in the waiting room instead. Sumbul is admitted; her parents are speaking to the doctors. Mama and Baba are on their way.

Nadia was pregnant. Oh, no, no, no. I hope we didn't kill her baby. Oh, no, no, no. Not another child. No, please, no.

I press my temples. My head hurts. My throat is dry. The bandages feel stiff on my neck, on my forehead, on my knees. They told me to take up a bed as well, but I refused.

I stand up shakily to go and find Nadia. It's true, she wasn't who I thought she would be. But I just want to see that she's okay now. Just this one last time, and then we can go on with our lives. Just to see if the baby is fine. Oh, God, please let the baby be fine.

I slowly go to the counter to enquire about her. I am at a loss for words.

"Th-There is a patient. Just got into a road accident. She's pregnant. May I know which room?" I ask the lady seated at the reception desk.

She looks up, uninterested. "Are you family?" she asks, sliding her glasses up her nose.

Am I family? I think for a moment. Nono in her uniform. Nono whispering in my ear. Nono eating *choran*. Nadia with her bloated belly.

"Yes. I-I'm family," I say.

NADIA

It seems like I have been adrift for two days. Somewhere under the shade of an okan tree, a graceful stream flowing, captivating me with its gushing water. I have been in and out of consciousness a few times, floating between serene silence and painful chaos. I know I am in a hospital. I know there was an accident. I feel like I have lost something.

How do I start counting my losses?

My baba, I shall count you first; you who silently faded away while I was growing in another city. Iqbal, you? Whom I loved dearly. I never thought you wouldn't get to be my children's uncle. Rocking them on your shoulders, buying them ice lollies. Abida, oh, dear Abida *bajjo*, your innocence? When did you lose that? On the fields? In the market? When you were taken away?

My amma, you never really received any respect from that house, did you? What did you do wrong? Your fault was that you brought me to Karachi?

My Misha, my *awal*. How I loved you. How I envied you. Whatever has happened to me in my life is my punishment. My

214

penance. I have not loved like I loved you. I have not lived like I lived with you.

I have spent my life chasing an ideal of what I should've become. I want to bring life into this world so I can be a better human being. I can bring up a girl in the world today who can stand on her own two feet. Someone who doesn't need to depend on anyone. I can bring up a girl who is educated, has a mind of her own, and will fight for her rights. I don't want her to be anyone's second choice, for she will always be my first choice.

To give birth is to crack something open. For something new to be created, something needs to rupture. The earth, an eggshell, a womb—to make way for life.

My loss is not what defines me. My mistakes are not what characterize me. I am not the difference between my past and my present. I am the sum of my experiences.

My body is beautifully numb. I open my eyes slowly to see where I am. There is a drip attached to my left hand. There is a catheter for my urine. There is a plaster on my right leg. There is a hard pillow placed under it. The sheets are stiff but clean. The bed is elevated slightly below my shoulders. My movement seems to be restricted. The room is brightly lit. On the side table is a bouquet of flowers. I close my eyes and open them again to see clearly. The card reads:

Get well soon
Best Wishes
Zohaib

The events of how I ended up here are blurry. I try to think back.

Gulshan guiding me onto an ambulance.

A collision.

I panic and look around. The room is empty. My belly is significantly reduced.

No. No. No. No!

I shut my eyes. *You deserve this.*

I'm sorry. I'm sorry. I'll be better. Just give me one last chance. I'll be better. *Ya Rabb*. I'll be better.

My loss feels heavy on my shoulders. My chest. My throat. My loss feels weightier than a mountain. Grief is sliding down my spine, my—

"Oh, *shukar. Shukar Khuda!* She's up!" Gulshan enters the room with a cast on her arm. Behind her is a nurse. In the nurse's arms is the most gorgeous sight I have ever laid my eyes upon. Bundled in a white hospital wrap is my love, my life, the light of my eyes, Misha. *My* Misha.

"Oh, good. Let's get you some food, baby bear," says the nurse.

"Let's get you some food," I croak, sobbing.

I take Misha in my arms. I see *her* in her eyes. A reflection, the same sparkle. Maybe I'm imagining it. Does life give you another chance? Has life given *me* a second chance?

I'll be better.

EPILOGUE

NADIA

Karachi, Pakistan

"Wake up, *gurya*, my *chand shehzadi*," Amma coos.

Misha pulls the cover over her head. She seems to be in the middle of a dream—a good one, from the look of bliss on her face. I roll my eyes. Of course, no nightmares for the princess.

"*Gurya raani*," Amma calls out lovingly, again in an attempt to wake her up.

I make a face. I've already been up for an hour, ironed my clothes, tried to rub off a stain from yesterday's curry. I've also folded my sheets, polished my shoes, and gobbled down a dry piece of bread.

"Masi! Don't spoil my dream!" Misha complains, opening one eye.

"Yes, yes, don't wake up her highness, the royal princess!" I blurt from the door, fully dressed, hair in a carefully made braid. I'm carrying my backpack on my shoulders and I'm ready to leave. My van driver picks me up first and drops me off last. I spend half my day with him. He stinks of *naswar* most days; I pinch my nose at the memory.

She suddenly opens both her eyes now and sits upright. She seems to have sensed me feeling superior this morning. She looks at me and gives Amma an exaggerated hug. I blow a raspberry at her.

"You want to drop me off downstairs?" I say coyly to Amma, in half Punjabi, half Urdu.

"*Na*, you go. I need to get Misha dressed; she's already running late," Amma says curtly, gesturing for me to go out. Her attention back towards Misha, her face breaks into a smile. "Toothbrush? Or should I put on your uniform first? Come on, lift your arms, there, there."

Misha lifts her arms, still in bed. Amma takes off her night shirt, and I avert my eyes. The last thing I need is to see Misha's upper body naked. I wear a trainer bra, but I'm pretty sure she doesn't.

I go down the steps and wait for the van to come. It will arrive at 7:50a.m. exactly, so I have three more minutes to kill. I put a finger in my nose to dig out this dry booger that has been bothering me, but, after careful searching, I seem to have scraped the inside of my nose. Yesterday, when Misha was picking her nose, Zohaib was saying, *Eugh! Disgusting!* So I also said, *Eugh! Disgusting!* Misha grunted at me and told me it's not like I never picked out a booger. I quickly take my finger out.

In the van, this boy, Suleman, always sticks his tongue out at me and always has sticky eyes. I look away and read the equations that Ms Anisa taught us in class. It's another standard day at school, except that Afifa calls me a *kutti* and I call her a *chootiya*, even though I don't really know what it means, but Shah Zaman *chacha* says it all the time.

When I come home, I go to have a shower. Misha is being fussed over by Bari *baji*—something about her hair not being shiny enough. *Boo hoo.*

When I come into Misha's room, Zohaib has his eyes covered.

"Get some clothes on, you naked girl!" he shrieks. I look down and see myself fully clothed.

"I'm trying to! Masi! Masi! My clothes! Towel!" Misha says it very loudly.

Now, Zohaib covers his ears, and his eyes are still closed. He looks funny. I crack up.

Zohaib squints one eye open and smirks at me. I instantly feel better about my day.

Amma rushes towards Misha, mollycoddling her again, so she can instantly get her dressed before Bari *baji* arrives on the scene.

"It's okay, Masi—relax. Just get me clothes. See, I'm almost dry." Misha touches her arm, and it's still wet.

I quickly hand Amma the towel, hoping for an appreciative nod, if nothing else. She ignores me and carries on dressing Misha.

Misha is dressed in her favourite pink T-shirt and denim shorts. Amma is now putting lotion on her arms and legs. I try to look unbothered, and go over to Zohaib instead.

Bari *baji* has been a little upset at Sahab. She keeps saying, "Your relatives, your relatives." I don't know who she's talking about. I try to remove myself from the situation whenever that is happening. I'm more interested in what Zohaib's plan is for the day.

"Misha! Look at your hair! Did you shower yourself? What a mess! There's still shampoo in it!" Bari *baji* says, now entering the room. She looks over at Amma accusingly, but doesn't say anything to her.

219

I feel bad that Amma is being scolded, but I don't know what I can do to help. I'll let Amma manage herself—after all, it serves her right for treating Misha like *her* baby all the time.

"What are we doing today?" I ask Zohaib quietly. I don't want any part of the commotion with Bari *baji* and her mood.

"Kite flying," he says, his eyes bright.

I open my eyes wide. Kite flying meant the roof, and the roof meant no Misha. I was more than ready for this plan; I could definitely use a break from her.

Later, Misha and I are playing with dolls. She gets the doll with the pretty blond hair, and I get the one with the shorter brown hair. I ask her for the blonde doll, but she refuses. She always has to get the better one. She *knows* I like the blonde one and on *purpose* makes me take the brown-haired one. I give her a moment to rethink her decision, but she just stares at me with blank eyes. I huff, put the brunette down and leave. Better to look for Zohaib. It's almost evening time, so, by my calculation, he should either be on the roof or on the staircase, preparing his kite. I pass by his room; he's not there.

I go into the kitchen and there is no one there either, since Shah Zaman *chacha* goes for a nap after lunch. I look on the veranda; Amma is lying down.

"Who is it?" She lifts her head, orange hair spilling out from her paisley-print dupatta.

"Where's Zohaib?" I ask her, although I know it's pointless. She won't know—or, worse, won't bother responding if she does.

"I don't know, maybe he has gone up to the roof," she says sleepily.

I look back to see if Misha is following me. I don't see her.

I quickly climb the stairs, some two at a time. When I reach the top, I'm excited and breathless. I open the heavy door to the roof.

The roof is large and mostly flat. There is some machinery up here—I think it's the generator, the big green thing. The sky is beautiful. It is strangely exhilarating to be up so high.

Zohaib is flying his favourite purple kite with green wings. It is a prized kite; I think he won it in a kite fight, where the neighbouring kids try to cut the thread of each other's kites. Once a thread has been cut, the chase is on to then run downstairs and claim your prize from wherever the kite has fallen. I walk over to him, smiling. He hands me the thread, and, just as he does so, I hear the roof door creak open.

Misha.

I knew she would be following me. Can't she be on her own for just a *minute*?

"Bhai, Bhai! Can I get a turn?" she asks Zohaib in her angelic voice.

"No! Misha, what are you doing here? You're not allowed here; Mama is going to be mad and blame me!" he says angrily.

"Then why is *she* here? *She's* also not allowed," she says accusingly, pointing her finger at me.

I shoot daggers at her with my eyes. She shrugs. Each girl for herself. She would never switch places with me, if she were holding the reel.

"She can at least hold the reel straight," Zohaib says, turning towards me. A pigeon flies by, really fast, causing him to duck. He looks at me; then, he looks at his kite.

The kite thread has been broken, Zohaib defeated. His kite is flying over, swaying in the light wind, this way and that. Zohaib is angry at Misha. I feel happy about that, but also a little sorry when I see her face drop.

The kite falls on the concrete overhang, next to our roof. It's a miracle it hasn't flown out on to the road. I start rushing towards it, and I see, from the corner of my eye, Misha has too.

She's climbing the low wall of the roof quickly. I know she's scared of heights; I run after her, not sure if I'm trying to save the kite or her. She's calculating her next move, I know—I've known her long enough. She's worried Zohaib will be mad at her. She just wants to hold the reel for him. The kite is stuck. I step onto the jetty, my back against the low wall of the roof. Misha is bending low, she's trying to reach for the kite, Zohaib's favourite. I stretch out my arm, lying flat, my heart beating so hard I can hear it.

Misha has closed in on the tail of the kite. I'm right behind her. She's tugging it gently to pull it free. Of course, she will reach the kite. Of course, she will rescue it. Of course, Zohaib will give her a bear hug and ask for forgiveness. Amma will come rushing up, Bari *baji* will embrace her. Misha, the perfect. Misha, the princess. I see myself behind my amma, smiling, clutching her leg, peeking at Misha, this beautiful foreign creature. I thought I had found a friend for life in this sweet angel, who would claim me as her friend, her sister, but I was never to be her equal.

She extends her hand; Misha is a step away from me now. She's without support, unstable on her feet kite in one hand. The ground is two floors down and it's concrete. I don't look down, but she does. Her eyes are wide and full of fear. She loses her balance. I'm shaking. The kite falls from her hand, and there is this thought: Did I take her hand? Why didn't I pull her in? Was it her shaking, or me? A barrage of memories appears in my vision suddenly. At the door, in the kitchen, on the veranda, on the jetty, in my loose-fitting school uniform, Shah Zaman, Iqbal's flaring nostrils, Abida *bajjo*, the blonde doll, the mulberry tree I never got to climb. The kite is flying, Misha is flying, Misha is falling.

"I'm sorry," I whisper into the air.

GLOSSARY

acha—okay/good

angrez—English speaking/white person

aray—hey

astaghfirullah—Arabic word for "I seek forgiveness in Allah"

azan—call for prayer

bacha / bachey—child

baji—older sister

bajjo—older sister

barey-barey—big-big/great-great

bas—enough

bhai—older brother

bhang—leaves used as a narcotic

bechari—poor girl

beta—son/daughter

begums—women belonging to a higher socio-economical class

bua—father's sister

chaand—moon; also a word of endearment

chacha—uncle/elder male

chachi—aunt; father's brother's wife

chaddar—large piece of cloth

chal—go

chalia—awalada, a digestive stimulant that may contain narcotics

chalo—let's go

chand—moon

chand shehzadi—a term of endearment that literally means "moon princess"

charpoy—bed made of strings

cheeku—naseberry, a type of fruit found in South Asia

chorangi—traffic roundabout

chuna—making a fool/load of rubbish

choti—small

chootiya—idiot/asshole

chorun—coloured candy

chupkar—shut up

awaladar—gatekeeper

chapal—slippers

daalchawal—lentils and rice, a South Asian dish

dadajee—paternal grandfather

dai—a midwife

dari—thickly woven floor mat

dars—religious sermon

dhaba—a roadside food stall

djinn—ghost

doodhpatti—tea beverage that originates from South Asia, milk and tea leaves are brought to a boil

dupatta—a long piece of cloth worn around the head, neck and shoulders, worn by women of South Asia

Eidi—money given as gift on Eid, a Muslim tradition

emaan—faith

Fajr—dawn prayer

Gajar ka bharta—roasted and mashed carrot

gurya—doll

gurya raani—doll princess, a term of endearment

haan—yes

haram—forbidden by Islamic law

hawaladar—a police officer reporting to a sergeant

Isha—night prayer

jaanu—my love

ji/jee—yes

jora—garment

jori—pair

kameez—shirt

kaamchor—shirk/lazy

kaki—aunt, a term used for older women out of respect

karakchai—strong tea

kasamse—I swear/I promise

khala—aunt

Khudahafiz—may God be your guardian

Kisay da yaar na wichray—famous Pakistani song, literal meaning: "may your love never leave you"

kulfi—a type of ice-cream originating from South Asia, usually in the shape of a cone

kurta pyjama—a collarless shirt worn over tailored pants by South Asian men

kutti—bitch

lehnga—a full-length skirt worn by South Asian women in celebratory events

maaf karo—forgive me

mahal—mansion or palace

mamu—maternal uncle

maulvi sahab—Quran teacher/person who reads the adhan

makai—baked corn

makaiwala—corn seller

Maghreb—evening prayer

manja—glass-powder coated string used for flying a kite

mano salva—the food sent down to Bani Israel, according to the Quran

marla—measurement used in South Asia, equal to about thirty square yards.

masi—helper/maid/aunt; literally translated as "like-mother," but usually used for domestic help in South Asia

memsahab—title of a woman in a place of authority

merijaan—my love/life

muhalla—locality/community

na—right/no

nafs—spirit/soul

nahin—no

naiki—good deed

nakhras—being picky or choosy

na-mehram—a man who is not related to a woman by blood or marriage

nankhatai—shortbread biscuits originating from South Asia

napaak—filthy

nasha—intoxication

naswar—a kind of dipping tobacco*pakka*—for sure

police waalas—policemen

purdah—hide/hide flaws

Rabb—God

rehmat—divine blessing

reham—kindness

rickshawwalas—rickshaw drivers

Rishta aunties—women in South Asian cultures who facilitate arranged marriages *roti*—flat round bread, cooked on a griddle

roza—fasting

saggi mother—real mother

sahab—sir

sanduk—metal suitcase

shalwar—loose trousers

shukar—thankfulness

shukriya—translates as "thank you"; Olivia Shukriya was a campaign led by a Pakistani beauty brand

tasbih—incantation of religious phrases/words for strength

taweez—a religious thread used for protection from evil

titlee—butterfly

thaila—a plastic or cloth bag

suno—listen

utho beta, Aankhen kholo—rhyme for children, literally meaning "wake up, open your eyes"

uff—an exclamation used when someone is annoyed, surprised, exhausted

wattasatta—a tradition that involves the simultaneous marriage of a brother–sister pair from one household to a sister–brother pair from another. It literally means "give–take"

wujud—existence

wuzu—ablution

ya Rabbi—oh Lord

zamindar—landowner

Zuhr—afternoon prayer

LIST OF CHARACTERS,
IN ORDER OF APPEARANCE

Nadia, nicknamed Nado/Nono—grew up as the daughter of the house help in the Hashim household

Shadab *sahab*—Nadia's boss

Mubashir—Nadia's (ex-)husband

Uzma—Nadia's colleague

Misha—daughter of Masood and Faiza, Zohaib's sister

Faisal—Nadia's work colleague

Zohaib, nicknamed Zo—son of Masood and Faiza, Misha's brother

Dr. Whitaker—Zohaib's therapist

Talha—Zohaib's best friend

Masi/Amma—Nadia's mother

Masood Hashim—father of Zohaib and Misha, a successful Karachi businessman

Faiza Usman—mother of Zohaib and Misha, married to Masood Hashim

Gulshan, nicknamed Goshi—Nadia's cousin who grew up with Nadia's family in the village after being orphaned as a child

Abida—Nadia's elder sister

Iqbal—Nadia's elder brother

ACKNOWLEDGEMENTS

I realized recently that I enjoy writing acknowledgements thoroughly. I owe deep gratitude to my parents, Ammi and Abbu, who have always, always believed in me, cheered me on, and celebrated my writing. I couldn't have finished this manuscript without Wajiha Hyder, who was a constant support while I was developing the plot. She has been as invested in the characters as I have been. I owe Mehr F. Hussain, without whom this book would not have found a home.

I am grateful to Archna Sharma for putting trust in my work. She has championed publishing diverse voices and I am happy she chose mine. Extending my thanks to Sofia Rehman for her erudite insights and astute suggestions to make this book the best version of itself. Gratitude to Lisa Cohen, who contributed some valuable observations and helped me find lustre in my story. It has been a beautiful journey and I'm glad my teammates were of the best kind.

No book is complete without the support of family; I appreciate my parents-in-law, especially Abujee, for the pride they take in my writing. My best friends, Zarmina Faisal Salman and Zahra Athar, for being voices of reason in my life.

Without sounding sappy, I would like to thank my partner in everything, Danish, for being my cheerleader always, for pushing me to do things I wouldn't have otherwise indulged in. Thank you for being my pillar. Two pieces of my heart, Aleesha and Affaan, this book is for you.

And, Dear Reader, thank you. Without you, I wouldn't be writing.